GOTHIC NOVELS

GOTHIC NOVELS

Advisory Editor:
Dr. Sir Devendra P. Varma

THE
NOCTURNAL MINSTREL

OR

THE SPIRIT OF THE WOOD

ELEANOR SLEATH

Introduction by Devendra P. Varma

ARNO PRESS

A New York Times Company
in cooperation with
MCGRATH PUBLISHING COMPANY

New York—1972

Reprint Edition 1972 by Arno Press Inc.

Special Contents Copyright © 1972 by Devendra P. Varma

LC#   70-131342
ISBN 0-405-00821-X

Gothic Novels
ISBN for complete set: 0-405-00800-7
See last page of this volume for titles.

Manufactured in the United States of America

Introduction

This elusive gothic novelist had baffled many researchers. Her *Orphan of the Rhine* (1798) is one of the Horrid Novels referred to by Jane Austen in *Northanger Abbey*. But her best work is perhaps *The Nocturnal Minstrel,* or *The Spirit of the Wood,* a romance in 2 vols, printed at the Minerva Press for A. K. Newman & Co., and published at Leadenhall Street in 1810.

This rare work has a talismanic power. Poetic in style, and very successful in creating a sense of atmosphere, Eleanor Sleath was courageous in attempting a period novel, and here she reveals her special knowledge of the panoply of chivalry. Despite the descriptions of the ivy-crusted turrets of the castle bathed in silvery moonlight, the shadows under the rustling leaves and the sleepy twitter of the martlet, several chapters of this novel sparkle with lively and dramatic dialogue. There emerges a ready wit and a hitherto unsuspected sense of humour. Gifted with a superior literary style set with glittering gems of descriptive power, she remains an enthusiastic lover of sensibility.

As a novelist, Mrs. Sleath stands midway between Mrs. Regina Maria Roche and Mrs. Eliza Parsons, but perhaps more incandescent than the former with an impassioned aptitude for gory scenes and a strong inclination towards paroxysmal adventures. Her love episodes rival those of Roche, and her characterisation, setting and decor are more artistically handled than those of Mrs. Parsons. In the art of embellishing her landscape settings, Mrs. Sleath is more sedulous and more

meticulous than Mrs. Roche, and stands as a contrast to the
often slatternly and conventional techniques of Mrs. Parsons.

She also wrote *Who's the Murderer,* or *The Mystery of
the Forest* (1802); *The Bristol Heiress* (1809); *Pyrenean
Banditti* (1811) and *Glenoven* (1815). *The Nocturnal Minstrel* or *The Spirit of the Wood* (1810) is a work of last
rarity. It is not in the famous Sadlier-Black Collection of
Virginia.

In their respective religious tenets, Mrs. Sleath and Mrs.
Parsons stand diametrically opposite to each other: whereas
the latter was apt to be "pugnaciously protestant", Mrs. Sleath's
ecclesiastical figures are all of noble and virtuous pattern, sane
and wise and spiritually inclined. This indicates that Mrs.
Sleath had strong leanings toward Roman Catholicism.

Catholic materials had come to provide the soupçon of
terror in gothic fiction by evoking scenes of "monastic gloom".
Catholicism also provided the *mise-en-scene* where brutal
figures could indulge in darkest deeds; where dreadful and
excruciating punishments were inflicted upon unfortunate,
often innocent victims. The figures of the penitent Nun and
the pious Abbess, the trembling Novice and the holy Father,
were often balanced against those dark and sombre characters.

In gothic fiction, therefore, Catholicism was not as an
actuality, but served as a means to evoke an atmosphere
leading to melodramatic situations and scenes of terror. Characters that flit across the dismal gloom of ecclesiastical ruins or
fill in the horrors of a religious recess, or spectres that glide
along chapel aisles, had powers to arouse emotions of pious
terror mixed with religious awe.

Catholic materials were also infused into the adventure-
love-story elements in gothic fiction to provide a milieu for
the action. The subterranean passageways, convent cells,
monastic prisons, chambers of the Inquisition, churchyards and
burial vaults in the crypts of chapels or abbey churches were
all appropriate settings.

'Catholicism' in Eleanor Sleath is, however, of a different texture. She reveals a contemplative turn of mind, and a high sense of religion. There are, in her works, warm references to the Catholic faith. She appears to be very well acquainted with monastic rituals and her works suggest that to her, peace could be obtained only in the solitude of a cloister, in holy retirement, amongst the placid countenances of the sisters, their gentleness and humility. The smell of incense wafts from her pages, and we listen to the choral chants on pensive evenings. She appears to be particularly fond of vestments and ceremony. Even the funerals are described in all "catholic" details.

Dedicated to the Christian way of life, she was practical, and not without secular interests, high among which stood architecture and gardening. Passages in her novels indicate her thorough knowledge of the intricate workmanship of gothic architecture. She appears also to be well acquainted with the Italian art of the period of Renaissance.

The images that adorn her altars are sculptured saints and crucifixes. The rich escutcheon, the cross and the tombs with figures piously recumbent are familiar sights in her holy mansions of the dead. Features revealed in the portraits of blooming knights and beauteous damsels hanging in the gallery, are delineated by the statuary wrought on the monumental marble, fixed and stiffened in death.

There are hours of crowded events and scenes of hot passions and wild gallantry. Her tales are full of blood, strife, hate and love, suspicions and mistrust. Her dark shadows and lurid lights are all pregnant with a throbbing interest.

She transmits the spirit behind the gloom of the ruined cathedrals perched on the spurs of the Appenines, and evokes the sinister atmosphere enshrouding the antique castles hanging along the craggy precipices of the Rhine.

Mrs. Sleath is, like Radcliffe, a mistress of hints and suggestions. There are descriptions of dreary rides over barren heaths and rugged slopes among faded and leafless woods. There are word-paintings of gloomy forests, desolate castles, and of the fury of heavy rains and high winds. She can, again like Mrs. Radcliffe, impart deep tones to the hollow murmurs of the wind, and call up a shudder through a light trembling of the leaves.

Her discriminating eye for colour is manifest in her ability to reveal the exquisite beauty of a moss-grown stone, to shelter her scenes with the cool shade of old oaks and yews, and to express the placid peace of summer meadows. She can convey to paper the spirit of the seasons: the russet browns of autumn, the sparkle and glitter of winter frost. She can interpret the awe-inspiring gloom of still waters in dim caverns, the boisterous shout of the mountain torrent, and the smooth urgency of rivers running down through deep and picturesque gorges. In Eleanor Sleath's prose we perceive the soul of the poet.

Her education had not been neglected, and her works reveal a familiarity with Shakespeare and *Ossian*. It is a matter of note that *The Orphan of the Rhine* was published in the same year as the Lyrical *Ballads*. To the new generation of poets, Nature relieved the mind and elevated the soul above the narrow confines of the world. They saw the Creator in His works, and adored in silence the perfection of the whole. This change in sensibility finds reflection even in the prose works of the period.

Mrs. Sleath is imaginatively acquainted with romantic Italy. She captures the pastoral atmosphere of the gay season of the vintage, the rural sports, the shepherd's pipe and the distant sound of tinkling sheep-bells on the mountains. There are animated descriptions of simple rustics leading their herds of goats along rugged mountain paths. She brings to us the soft breathings of a flute and the melodious burst of the nightingale's song. In the scenic backdrop we see the vast range of the Alps with their towering summits lost in clouds.

She charms us also with scenes of serenity and tranquillity, when not a breath of air disturbs the calm, or shakes the lightest foliage of the trees standing against a dusky sky. And then, softened by distance, the silence of the evening is penetrated by a sweet and mournful cadence of the chant of the nuns from a lonely cloister.

The Orphan of the Rhine (1798) is an incredible tale, narrated in the language of sensibility and built on extravagant incidents. The advertisement to Vol. I mentions that this was Mrs. Sleath's first performance. This entertaining novel has been categorised as a Rochean romance, less rhapsodical and less lovely, but founded on virtue and sprinkled with good sense, and strangely attractive even in its absurdities.

Mrs. Sleath rings up the curtain on a grand scenic effect and a dramatic situation: in a deep, wooded valley of the Swiss Alps, the tall, elegant Julie de Rubine has the placid calm of her retired life shattered by the arrival of a carriage before the cottage where she resides with her infant son, Enrico. From the equipage there alights 'a tall, thin woman of unhealthy appearance' who, acting for the powerful Marchese de Monteferrat, leaves in Julie's care an infant girl, named Laurette, an orphan but four months old. She also hands to Julie a letter from the Marchese, ordering her to leave Switzerland and take up her abode, with the two children, in the Castle of Elfinbach on the Rhine.

The journey enables Mrs. Sleath to employ the full orchestra of her powers: in addition to a running description of the changing scene, she introduces incidents of overwhelming drama, mystery and suspense. At a lonely inn on a desolate mountain pass Julie meets a gaunt and ailing traveller named La Roque who is fleeing from the diabolical Marchese de Monteferrat.

The Castle of Elfinbach appears to have some shades of Udolpho about it: it is situated in dense, impenetrable woodland overlooking the deep, broad, silent flowing Rhine. Its turrets and pinnacles, crumbling with age and neglect, are in part ruinous; the wind howls mournfully through corridors, agitating the tapestries, and adding menace to the sinister atmosphere of the place. Weeds sprout from cracks in the massive walls, and spring from between the flag-stones in the courtyard where there stands an equestrian statue, the description of which, as soft moonlight silvers its contours, reveals the author's artistry.

We are not left to wonder why Julie de Rubine unresistingly obeys the commands of the Marchese: we learn that he had trapped her into a mock marriage, and that Enrico is his illegitimate son. Julie, thinking she hears groans and the clank of chains coming from a dilapidated wing of the Castle of Elfinbach, sets out to investigate and, to her horror, finds, chained to the wall of a dark dungeon, the emaciated figure of a man. It is La Roque whom she had met at the desolate inn, when journeying to Elfinbach.

Released from captivity by Julie, La Roque takes sanctuary in a local monastery and his story is revealed. He is the Count de la Croisse who, having been left an orphan, was reared by the previous Marchese de Monteferrat whose daughter, Helena, he had ultimately married.

Immediately before her mock marriage, Julie, living in Italy had been courted by a young gallant named Vescolini who, it now transpires, was La Roque's son, assassinated in the streets of Naples by instigation of the Marchese de Monteferrat.

The author reverts to her main theme and introduces a series of surprising incidents: Julie is kidnapped, and Laurette is conducted from Elfinbach to another castle which is situated in Salzburg. Her guide is Paoli, the confidential servant and unscrupulous agent of the evil Marchese de Monteferrat. The news of Julie's disappearance reaches Enrico who rides immediately to his mother's aid. At the Castle of Elfinbach where he expects to get information, his hopes are dashed: the only reply to his knocking is the hollow echo that rebounds from the deserted building. Mrs. Sleath here makes a most impressive use of contrasting sounds and silence which she brings to a climax with the clatter of the horse's hoofs as Enrico, baffled, eventually rides away. Late at night, riding through forest land he is attracted by a light and finds it is a lamp burning in a decayed hunting-lodge. Enrico knocks and is admitted by a haggard, unsavoury and uncommunicative person whose dagger, visible among the rags with which he is clothed, is rusted with blood. During the night, while his host sleeps, Enrico takes the lamp and makes a cautious search of the building. On a mattress in the corner of one of the rooms he sees a still, veiled, feminine form, who proves to be Laurette, who has been brought there to be murdered.

The author, feeling that it is time to bring the long, complex story to an end, does so by the simple process of recalling La Roque, who informs Enrico that his mother is safe in a convent, and advises him to return with Laurette to the Castle of Elfinbach. Upon arrival, Enrico finds the Marchese on his death-bed, filled with remorse and repentance. His last act is to join the hands of the hero and the heroine and give them his blessing.

Mrs. Sleath uses the flash-back device in her first novel, and such conventional gothic trappings as the locked wings of the castle, in the manner of Clara Reeve's *Old English Baron* (1777). Like Radcliffe, she also contrives to explain the phantoms and the supernatural. Although *The Critical Review* of November 1799 condemned this novel as "a vapid and servile imitation" of "the creative genius and the descriptive powers of Mrs. Radcliffe", the scenes of complicated guilt and depravity are wonderfully unfolded.

Character portrayal is convincing, and physical features are invariably appropriate: the friar has a thin aesthetic face furrowed with age and patiently borne afflictions; the villainous Paoli is stocky and stern, harsh and forbidding, his searching glance inducing anxiety, and none can feel at ease in his presence. Perhaps one traces in him shades of Radcliffe's Schedoni.

The Marchese de Monteferrat emerges as a passionate and diabolical character. A person of restless inquietude, his discoloured imagination is rendered still more dreary by his mournful solicitude. His dark, piercing eyes sparkle with ferocity and dread. He leaves an unforgettable impression and stands out vividly in a number of scenes. We find his reflection in the Venetian mirror of Laurette's chamber, his cloak hanging loosely from his shoulder, his plumes waving haughtily over his brow, his darkened countenance strongly marked with rage, jealousy and revenge. We discover him sitting with a lamp and a book, reposing in a large antique chair by the dying embers of the fire on a winter night. Denied slumber, passing sleepless nights wrapped in the gloom of silent thoughts, his guilty soul conjures up strange and dreadful images.

In *The Orphan of the Rhine* the secondary themes are well integrated with the main plot, and do not burst obtrusively into the story. Mrs. Sleath, being overgenerous, crowds too many gems together but they do not overwhelm or obliterate each other, while the sterling qualities of the work are high enough to cover all faults and blemishes. Eleanor Sleath's own genius was pouring its strong beams out through her maiden effort.

Mrs. Sleath followed this popular novel with *Who's the Murderer?, or The Mysteries of the Forest* (1802), a work in four volumes, published by the Minerva Press. The story opens in a dramatic manner: a wretched female, abandoned to the heaviest of misfortunes and the fatigue of a very long journey, is seeking shelter at an unknown door. She happens to be the widow of a Gascon soldier who had succumbed to wounds, and to add to her misfortunes, she has been robbed by banditti of the Pyrenees.

A ruined mansion in the forest where eventually she seeks asylum with a stranger, is the haunt of marauders. A hunter brings a sack, and the horrific discovery of the body of a newly murdered man is made. The narrative centres on the mystery of the birth of Cecilia, to be unravelled in the end by caskets and parchment scrolls. The scenes shift through landscapes in Naples, Genoa, Florence, Pisa and Provence.

The author artistically evokes in night and silence the solemn pomp which waits on the last melancholy incident in the life of man. Solemn funeral processions steal through dreary arches. The glare of torches in the silent mansions of the dead, the vault surrounded with coffins and tombs, grim and ghost-like figures holding tapers or supporting crucifixes—all these create nightmarish sensations:

> As she advanced again from the door, she thought the figures on the coffins began to move; their marble features became fleshy—the lights they held waxed pale—a strong sulphurous vapour rose from the tombs . . . She made an effort to depart; but her feet, when she would have moved, sunk imperceptibly into the ground—a hot boiling fluid seemed to be gathering around them—and in a moment she was involved in a sea of blood!

The dreary eloquence of the prisoner in the tower pulses with desperation:

> For what is it I live? To be the companion of the dead—the inhabitant of a dreary and deserted turret—to watch the faint radiance of the sun as it dawns through its grated apertures—to chide its lingering beams as it sets beyond the high and trackless mountain—to hear no sound but the wind as it breaks in sudden gusts over my head, or the hoarse voice of my keeper as he stalks across my chamber.

Through a maze of adventures, the story concludes in ungoverned ecstasies and transports of joy, in the union of Varano and Cecilia.

Her next work, *The Bristol Heiress or The Errors of Education,* is a long novel in five volumes, published by the Minerva Press in 1809. Although the opening chapters contain a long discourse on the female education of the times, the story unfolds gorgeous scenes of the life of the eighteenth century aristocracy with all its opulence and dissipation, its gaming tables and card-parties. The magnificence of aristocratic homes is revealed in their costly carpets and gilded sofas, their luminous chandeliers reflected in large mirrors lining the walls, their carriages and liveried servants and trains of black slaves. Ladies are seen sweeping their long Indian muslin robes across the room with an irresistible air of fashion, and English peeresses are loaded with the splendours of rank and nobility.

It is a tale of civilized society, and it is not until the last volume, when the scene shifts to Borrowdale Castle in Cumberland, that the colouring takes a gothic mood and tone, and we hear of the ghost of the murdered wife of Lord Aldibert, dressed in a long white robe, all spattered with blood and bearing in her hand a lighted taper.

Mrs. Sleath's best work is perhaps *The Nocturnal Minstrel; or The Spirit of the Wood,* a romance in two volumes, printed at the Minerva Press for A. K. Newman & Co., and published at Leadenhall-Street in 1810. The story centres on the Baroness Gertrude Fitzwalter, a beautiful rich widow of twenty-three, the sole possessor of an ancient, gloomy castle situated among wilds and mountains. There she lives alone, her only companions being her vassals and domestic servants.

Sometimes in the hush of a calm night the enchanting melody of a lute is heard from the surrounding woods, flooding the atmosphere with ecstatic sweetness. Efforts to locate this mysterious minstrel had proved fruitless, and the music came to be associated with the supernatural. No one could muster courage to wander near the woods after dusk had fallen.

Reports of the spectral visitant accumulate; nor are the appropriate atmospheric conditions—clouded moonlight, wind and storm—wanting to these manifestations.

The novelist, here describes an elaborate pageant of chivalry. It is interesting to note that the details are of the typical 'historical' kind, and is it possible that Eleanor Sleath could have successfully manufactured historical romances, had she tried her hand in that direction.

Eleanor Sleath wrote *Pyrenean Banditti,* a romance in three volumes, which was published by the Minerva Press in 1811. The story opens in wild Gascony in the middle of the seventeenth century, and the setting is an inaccessible castle commanding a view of deep and extensive valley, rich with dark pine woods and narrow glens opening among the Pyrenees. The castle is surrounded by a broad moat, now silted up; the entrance is by way of a drawbridge. It is the home of an avaricious Count of haughty and tyrannical disposition, who neither retains the opulence nor possesses the virtues of his ancestors. He spends his days mostly in Paris in the dissipations of that voluptuous city, and having squandered his fortunes, at the age of forty, he marries the widow of a rich Portuguese merchant, past the bloom of life but amiable and attractive.

During his early youth, the Count had attempted to entice a rich young heiress, had offered himself as her lover, but was rejected. Instead, the lady married his brother, the Chevalier St. Augouléme, whom the Count detested as the rival of his hopes and ambitions. The Count never forgave this injury. After a decade the Chevalier, suffering from nervous disorder, and advised to travel, arrives at the castle with his daughter Adelaide, a charming girl of seventeen, and makes the Count and Countess joint executors and guardians of his daughter's person and property, in the event of· his own death. Adelaide's personal graces are described, her ease and dignity of manners, and the power of her charm.

The Chevalier, having caught cold in one of the evening rides, dies a few weeks later, in the arms of his beloved daughter. The Count's thoughts centre upon the greatest possible advantage to be made of the power vested in him by the will of his late brother as the guardian of his niece's property and person.

Adelaide had long perceived the traces of a concealed grief in the countenance and manners of her aunt—and one day she discovered the cause. When the Countess had decided to keep half of her property for her orphan nephew, Theodore, she was virtually made a prisoner in the castle because of her refusal to sign the papers. Theodore gets a commission in the army, but is asked never to visit the castle again. Even Adelaide's claim to the property of the late Chevalier came to be questioned, for it was rumoured in various parts of Provence that she was not the legitimate daughter of the Chevalier.

About three leagues away was the Castle of Ponteville, reputed a haunted place. At twelve in the night, lights appeared at the windows, and a ghost wrapped in a bloody sheet was seen stalking about the apartments. One solemn evening, a traveller had seen the western side of the edifice illuminated. Two persons who had ventured to enter had perished.

Adelaide, kidnapped by two masked ruffians, finds herself a prisoner in the castle. Here she has spectral experiences, but ultimately escapes. She becomes the innocent victim of villainous plots, but she faces all her vicissitudes with the calm courage typical of a romantic heroine.

The Castle of Ponteville, long abandoned by the owners to neglect, became the resort of robbers whose artifices effectually prevented the intrusion of all prying visitors and established the belief that it was haunted by horrible and dangerous spectres. The story ends in the marriage of Theodore and Adelaide.

Her published works stretch over a period of seventeen years. It remains, however, to ascertain whether she died in or soon after 1815, the date of the publication of her last novel *Glenoven, of The Fairy Palace*. Or whether she survived long afterwards and laid by her pen, having taken to retirement like the 'Mighty Magician of the Mysteries of Udolpho'.

Her works do indicate a particular fascination for Germany, the country of necromantic tales and superstitious legends. She may be resting in splendour for eternity in some endeared spot: perhaps on the bank of the Rhine, the most haunted river of the world, in some desolate cemetery in the vicinity of a German castle hanging on a precipitous cliff; or lying in eternal sleep on the fringe of the Black Forest which abounds in legends of Demon Huntsmen, witches and werewolves; or buried in Salzburg, famed for its sacred wells, superstitious magic and ancient lore. Yet from the depth of her unspotted tomb, her empty sarcophagus, may still be rising the scent of herbs, cedar oil, resin and myrrh. Yet when the *Apfelbaum-bluten* blossom in the German countryside bursting into flakes of rosy loveliness, their short spell of glorious flowering is appropriate to the transient popularity of Eleanor Sleath, the 'veiled-mistress' and 'phantom queen' of gothic romance.

Dalhousie University   *Devendra P. Varma*
Nova Scotia

Select Bibliography

I. GENERAL

Birkhead, Edith. *The Tale of Terror.* 1921.

Railo, Eino. *The Haunted Castle.* 1927.

Tompkins, J. M. S. *The Popular Novel in England (1770-1800).* 1932.

Praz, Mario. *The Romantic Agony.* 1933.

Summers, Montague. *The Gothic Quest.* 1938.

Varma, Devendra P. *The Gothic Flame.* 1957.

II. SPECIAL

Blakey, Dorothy. *The Minerva Press* (1790-1820). 1939.

Tarr, Sister Mary Muriel. *Catholicism in Gothic Fiction.* 1946.

Mayo, Robert D. *The English Novel in the Magazines (1740-1815).* 1962.

Levy, Maurice. *Le Roman "Gothique" Anglais (1764-1824).* 1968.

III. ON ELEANOR SLEATH

Varma, Devendra P. Introduction to Eleanor Sleath's *Orphan of the Rhine* published by Folio Press London (The Northanger set of The Seven Horrid Novels). 1968.

THE

NOCTURNAL MINSTREL.

—

A ROMANCE.

Lane, Darling, and Co. Leadenhall Street.

THE

NOCTURNAL MINSTREL;

OR,

THE SPIRIT OF THE WOOD.

A Romance.

———◦◦◦◦◉◦◦◦———

———◦◦◦◦◉◦◦◦◦———

BY MRS. SLEATH,

AUTHOR OF

THE ORPHAN OF THE RHINE, WHO'S THE MURDERER?
BRISTOL HEIRESS, &c. &c.

Can any mortal mixture of earth's mould,
Breathe such divine enchanting ravishment?
Sure something holy lodges in that breast,
And with these raptures moves the vocal air,
To testify his hidden residence!
How sweetly did they float upon the wings
Of Silence, through the empty vaulted night,
At every fall smoothing the raven down
Of Darkness, till it smil'd.

MILTON.

———»»◉««———

LONDON:

PRINTED AT THE
Minerva-Press,
FOR A. K. NEWMAN AND CO.
(Successors to Lane, Newman, and Co.)
LEADENHALL-STREET.
1810.

THE
NOCTURNAL MINSTREL.

CHAP. I.

That strain again!—it had a dying fall;
Oh, it came o'er my ear like the sweet South,
That breathes upon a bank of violets,
Stealing and giving odour.

SHAKESPEARE.

"OH, how enchanting are those notes!
surely some being from a happier world—
some spirit, or some heavenly chorister,
visits these woods, to charm us with
celestial minstrelsy! Listen, Winifred,
but do not speak: Oh, what a swell was
there, and what a cadence!"

B   Such

Such were the exclamations uttered at intervals by the Baroness Fitzwalter, as she sat in her oriel, during the twilight hours of a summer eve, listening to the sounds of some unknown minstrel, which had then lately frequented the woods, covering the hills around the castle— sounds which came floating with bewitching sweetness over the waters of the lake which washed the base of the tower in which she sat, and died away in lingering echoes, reverberated from the opposite and rather distant rocks.

"Indeed, Lady," said her attendant Winifred, when the music had ceased for awhile, "the minstrel, whoever he is, is right cunning in his craft."

"Have you punctually obeyed my orders," resumed the Baroness; "is it sufficiently known throughout my domains,

6   that

that I offer a large reward for the discovery
of this invisible musician? that I would
gladly give him, could I see him, a thankful
recompence, for the entertainment he has
already afforded me? and even, should he
be inclined to accept it, a permanent
establishment in this castle?"

"Yes, Lady, these your orders have
been published, but with no effect. This
minstrel is heard, but never seen; from
which it is plain, he either cannot or will
not shew himself."

"How! cannot!"

"Why, Lady, if it is a spirit—"

"A spirit, Winifred!"

"If it is a spirit that haunts the woods,
he may not perhaps have the power, even
if he had the will, to assume a human
shape, or indeed any shape whatever; for
a spirit, they say, is nothing but air; and

if

if he could, he would probably have no mind to accept your Ladyship's offers to come and live with us at the castle."

"Nor, under such circumstances," answered the Baroness, smiling, "should I desire his presence.—But soft, the music comes again, and seems, or my senses deceive me, to advance still nearer. Go, bid the seneschal step out and meet the stranger, and in courteous guise invite him to enter my walls."

"Hark!" cried Winifred, "did not you hear a rustling under yon trees?"

"I did," answered the Baroness, "but yet I believe it might be only fancy."

"And did you not see somebody there?"

"I saw what seemed like something; but it was only the moonlight shadow of the yew beside the bridge."

"The

" The music stopped as you spoke, yet
I heard no step.—It is very strange."

" More than a week has elapsed," said
the Baroness, " since this mysterious
minstrel first began his nightly wanderings through these woods; and yet, in all
that time, though you assure me the most
diligent search has been made for his discovery, nothing is or can be known about
him. Sometimes when all is hushed,
when not a breeze ruffles the lake, or
shakes the lightest foliage of the trees, the
enchanting melody of that lute has broke
upon the silence of the night, in tones of
such extatic sweetness, that all my senses
have been wrapt in wonder and delight!
And I have thought, Winifred, for at
times I could scarcely allow myself to
think the strings of the instrument, whose
sweet tones enchanted my ear, and seemed

to

to wrap my soul in a temporary delirium, were touched by mortal hand, I have thought, that in approbation of the resolution I have long formed of devoting my days to widowhood, and the remembrance of a husband's love, some benignant—some approving spirit hovers near me, perhaps that of my long-regretted Lord."

" I should sooner think, Lady," answered Winifred, " supposing the musician to be a spirit, the spirit of the noble Baron, he would sooner persuade you to throw aside your mourning weeds, and elect another happy bridegroom in his stead, than advise you to pine in hopeless grief, as you now do, for a husband whom all your sorrow cannot bring to life again."

" I know, Winifred," cried the Baroness, " that all my grief is unavailing; it cannot,

cannot, as you say, bring him back to me."

"Why, then, Lady, suffer it to take such deep root in your heart? It is now near thirteen months since the news of the Baron's death, after an absence of near two years, first reached the castle, and you are still drowned in tears for his loss, as though the event was but of yesterday."

"Can I weep too long for such a husband? was he not all that my fond heart could wish, noble, generous, and brave?"

"He was, my Lady; but he is dead and gone, and out of so many lovers——"

"I am unable," interrupted the Baroness, "to find one, were I so inclined, that I could even bear to think of as a husband."

"Had I the choice amongst them,"

cried

cried Winifred, " I should not long deliberate: the young knight, Sir Reginald Harcland."

" You are always naming this Sir Reginald, Winifred," said the Baroness.

" He is surely the handsomest man in England," resumed Winifred, " and the most accomplished knight. He rides distinguished at the tournaments, and dances charmingly at the ball."

" He may be all this," cried the Baroness, " and even more, and yet I cannot love him."

" The greater your misfortune, Lady, for I am sure he loves you."

" I am somewhat doubtful on this point, Winifred," pursued the Baroness.

" Doubtful! what, when he has declared it over and over again! when he swears he cannot live without you! when he is mad

mad almost with extasy at the very sound of your voice, and looks (oh how my heart has ached for him!) as wan as a ghost when you have spoke coldly to him!"

" He can sigh, indeed, Winifred," cried the Baroness, " most profoundly, and breathe the language of adoration at the feet of his imaginary idol, as well, or perhaps better, than any man in Christendom. He can look, too, most woe-begone. But these, Winifred, are not always the certain indications of true passion; all this may be assumed: yet supposing he does love me, how can I give him my hand, when he is unable to excite in me the same sensations which he himself feels? would not this be folly?—nay, would it not be madness? I am weary of his complaints and importunities; his perseverance is intolerable!"

" There

" There is but one way, Lady,"returned Winifred, " by which you can effectually secure yourself from the solicitations of a love so sincere and so ardent as that of Sir Reginald."

" I would know it then," cried the Baroness, " for in troth I am most heartily weary of him, and would give any thing to be rid of such a troublesome suitor."

" You must marry him then, Lady.

" Ah there. Winifred, you are right; the lover would soon be lost in the husband; but in that case the remedy would be even more painful than the disease of which I complain. As the kinsman of my late Lord, he has claims upon my respect; yet of late he has become presuming—I had almost said impertinent; and I must positively invent some scheme

to

to put an end to his present hopes, if he is still absurd enough to entertain any, and without any absolute rudeness on my part, drive him from my castle."

"How, Lady!" exclaimed Winifred, "drive him from your castle! drive Sir Reginald from your castle! surely, my Lady, my dear, my noble, my honoured Lady, you cannot mean to be so cruel! why, he would fall upon his own sword, or throw himself from some frightful precipice; and how could you endure to think of him, all mangled and bloody, or bear to see him, as you perhaps might, should his spirit (holy St. Agatha protect it!) not rest in its grave, entering your chamber in the dead of night, his face pale as ashes, his eyes rolling in anger, wakening you from a blessed sleep to be terrified with the dreadful vision!—and

then

then tempt you bewildered to follow it
into some low deep cave in the rocks, or
into the darkest recesses of the woods!
Oh horrible, horrible, Lady! you will not
sure drive him to despair—you will not
allow yourself (I am sure I could not)
to have to answer for being the cause of
his death! No, no, no, my Lady."

"Oh, never fear," cried the Baroness
calmly, "he is too much attached to his
own dear person, to disfigure it with a
mortal wound; nor will he let his grief,
at what you call my cruelty, in any
degree hurt his health. But I cannot
live thus continually exposed to the
importunities of a man, whose behaviour becomes irksome to me; he must
therefore, and you, Winifred, may assist
me in devising the means, be dismissed
from this castle. In this we must, however,

ever, proceed with caution; for he is powerful in the number of his vassals, and in no little favour at court; and might therefore be dangerous, if much offended."

"Alas! poor Sir Reginald! who will tell him? It will be death, Lady, death at once."

"No more, Winifred" cried the Baroness; "will you never have done commiserating this foolish knight?"

"Oh, mercy on us!" cried Winifred. "His body, as I was saying, cut and mangled, pale, bleeding; his wounds, like so many mouths, opened to accuse you alone, all alone, by your bedside; the castle clock striking one; the sheet that wraps him sprinkled with his blood, half raised at the left arm, to shew the death-wound at his heart——"

"Prithee,

" Prithee, Winifred, make an end of thy horrible representations," cried the Baroness, " or with a little of thy imagination, aided by the lateness and gloominess of the present hour, I shall imagine I see a spectre gliding into some remote corner of my apartment. Methinks it already waxes late. What a clock is it, Winifred? I feel strangely wearied."

" It is near twelve, Lady; the castle clock has already struck the quarters."

" Leave me then to my repose," cried the Baroness; " perhaps the invisible minstrel—Ah! while I speak, the strain, as usual at the hour of midnight, comes sweetly swelling through the foliage of the woods! Retire, Winifred, I would be alone—I would feast upon the eloquence of of those soul-subduing sounds. Good night, and may the holy angels guard you !"

Winifred withdrew, and the Baroness retired to her bed : as she sunk upon her pillow, the music advanced nearer; it seemed almost to approach her window. The strain was sweet, but sad ; it became more and more plaintive; and as she listened in wrapt and silent attention, it seemed to come immediately under her casement. Not altogether uninfluenced by the late representations of her attendant, she listened, trembling lest some supernatural object should meet her eye; her heart beat quick; she trembled as she listened. At length, taking courage, she approached the window. She gazed around, but could discern nothing; for a heavy cloud had enveloped the broad disk

of

of the moon, and not a star twinkled in the sky. She even ventured to call;—no answer was returned. The music stopped when she had spoke; but the strain was quickly resumed: it grew fainter and fainter; the sounds receded toward the woods, died away in a sweet, but mournful cadence, and all around was hushed in silence. The Baroness won-dered—was astonished; but unable to account for these mysterious sounds, she returned to her bed, where she long lay lost in conjecture, and agitated by various surmises, till nature at length yielded to the stillness of the midnight hour, and she sunk as by necessity to sleep.

CHAP.

—————————

CHAP. II.

O mi Fortuna fella,
Che cambio e queste che tu fai!
ARIOSTO.

GERTRUDE, Baroness Fitzwalter, the occupier and now sole possessor of an ancient but magnificent castle, situate on an extensive demesne, not far from the Scottish border, between whom and her attendant the conversation we have just related passed, was the widow of Geoffry, Baron Fitzwalter, a nobleman highly distinguished by his personal qualities, and who, in birth, title, and extensive domains, ranked

ranked among the first of the nobility of
the age.

The Baron, during the reigns of Edward
the Fourth and the Usurper Richard, had
been a zealous partizan of the House of
York. Disgusted, however, by the crimes
and cruelties of the latter monarch, he had
not scrupled, on Henry's declaration of
his intention of uniting the interests of
the opposite families by a marriage with
the Princess Elizabeth, to offer him his
allegiance; and to enter into a further
alliance with the opponent party, by an
union with the heiress of the Barony of
Broke, a young lady, whose beauty and
various accomplishments, when in her
seventeenth year, (at which early age, in
compliance with the implied command of
the King, she gave her hand to the
Baron) had procured her a numerous
                                                  train

train of admirers, and caused her to be esteemed one of the brightest ornaments of the English Court.

Notwithstanding the arbitrary means used to effect their union, the most entire confidence and affection subsisted between the married pair; every succeeding year augmented their mutual attachment; and with the exception of the loss of an infant daughter, who had died a few weeks after its birth, no event occurred during the first years of their marriage to interrupt their happiness, or cloud the prospect of their future years.

The war between England and France, and the invasion of Britany by the English, first occasioned a temporary separation of the Baron and Baroness; for he, eager to signalize himself in the field of honour, was amongst those faithful adherents

rents of the reigning monarch, who, fond of the pride of war, and glowing with military ardour, had offered their services in his purposed invasion of France; little imagining that the shew of a siege at Boulogne was to terminate the achievements of the boasting King; and that avarice, and not glory, was with him the only motive of the expedition. From this period, though the Baron received many marks of favour and distinction from the politic Henry, he began to entertain a secret disgust toward his government. His neglect of the Queen, his cruel policy in respect to Warwick, who was then a close prisoner in the Tower, his rigorous treatment of the Queen-mother, the unfortunate widow of Edward the Fourth, his mean avaricious propensities, and the little regard he testified

fied for the honour and glory of the English nation, all conspired to estrange him from the court, and to produce a regret for having offered allegiance to so unworthy a monarch.

His disgust, however, for some time was no otherwise expressed than in remaining absent from court, and by inquiring, in common with other malcontents, whether the pretensions of Simnel, who was now practising his impostures in various parts of the kingdom, were founded in truth. But although the Baron was proof against the machinations and contrivances of the partizans of this pretender, he soon fell into a snare, not less injurious to his interests and his honour than that he had escaped. The imposture of Simnel was soon detected; the real Warwick was produced, and the disappointed spirit of faction

faction again sunk into repose. Perkin
Warbeck, concerning whose pretensions
historians are not even yet agreed, appeared in England, bearing the name and
title of Richard, Duke of York, and soon
became a formidable adversary to the
unpopular King.

Margaret, Duchess of Burgundy, had
recognized him as the second son of
Edward the Fourth, having professed her
belief in his declaration, that he had
escaped from the Tower, when his brother
the fifth Edward was murdered by Tyrrel,
at the instigation of the tyrant Richard.
This her conviction had obtained for this
Duke of York the countenance of the
King of France, and the support of the
greater part of the English malcontents;
for the Duchess had sent her emissaries
throughout the kingdom, to invite thither

such

such of the English nobility as had been known formerly to have attached themselves to the interests of the York party.

Of these, Geoffry, Baron Fitzwalter, was among the most forward in arms; for influenced by the representations of Clifford, Lord Viscount Lovel, and others, who had seen the pretended prince, he went secretly into Flanders. He was welcomed by Margaret with every demonstration of joy, and introduced to Warbeck, whom he no sooner beheld, than seduced by the striking resemblance he really bore to the royal Edward, to whom he (the Baron) had been always singularly attached, than he immediately acknowledged him as his rightful sovereign, and prepared to follow the fortunes of this daring adventurer.

The

The intrigues and system of espionage practised by the King, anticipated and prevented the serious attacks intended by his adversaries; and the distracted Baroness, to whom the real motive of the Baron's expedition to Flanders, and the consequences of it, were yet unknown, heard almost at the same instant of his death, and that an act of attainder had already passed, by which the Fitzwalter estates had become forfeit to the crown.

Through the solicitations and interference of Lord Broke, the father of the Baroness, who in every emergency had proved himself a steady and faithful adherent to the present monarch, this act of attainder was suspended, and permission granted the Baroness, to hold during her life the free possession of the demesne and

and estates of the house of Fitzwalter; on her death, they were to lapse to the crown.

This was an indulgence which, considering the jealous disposition of Henry, his insatiable avarice, and the decided antipathy he entertained towards the Yorkists, may appear somewhat extraordinary; but it was proved that the Baroness was not accessary, or in any way concerned in the treason for which the Baron was attainted; and the former services of her family being taken into consideration, who had all of them been active in the support of the Lancastrian interests, a further grant was passed, several months after the death of the Baron, enabling the Baroness, on certain conditions there specified, to transmit her possessions to her family.

c   CHAP.

———————

CHAP. III.

How does he love me?

With adorations, with fertile tears;

With groans that thunder love, with sighs of fire.

SHAKESPEARE.

IT was from her father, Lord Broke, that the Baroness first received the melancholy intelligence of the Baron's death; the particulars of it she had learned from Sir Reginald Harcland, a gentleman nearly related, on the maternal side, to the family of Fitzwalter, who had been long on terms of the most friendly intimacy with the late Baron, and from whom the Baro-

ness

ness herself had received many proofs of regard.

After the death of the Baron, as soon, and indeed sooner, than was consistent with the laws of delicacy and decorum. he became her professed admirer. But the Baroness, though she had respected him as a friend, and, owing to the connection which subsisted between the families, and his intimacy with the late Baron, had suffered him to pay her a visit of condolence a short time after his death, refused to receive him as a lover; nor could he, by any arts and expressions of tenderness and affection, vanquish. or undermine the steady and inviolable resolution she had formed, of rejecting every alliance that might offer, however noble and advantageous.

Young, ardent, and enterprizing, of a

disposition

disposition inclined to resist wayward circumstances, rather than to yield to them,
Sir Reginald could neither determine to
abandon the pursuit, or resolve to surmount the passion he felt for this emi-
nently lovely woman, who, had beauty
been her only charm, possessed a sufficient
portion of this quality, to have enslaved a
heart far less susceptible of its blandish-
ments than was that of Sir Reginald.

The Baroness pitied, and then reproved
the warmth of a passion she determined
to discourage; for she felt herself utterly
unable, independent of her resolve of continued widowhood, to make any return of
affection. To her, indeed, influenced as
she was by the remains of attachment for
her late lord, the extravagant expressions
of love made by Sir Reginald seemed
monstrous; nay, its very vehemence led
her

her to doubt its sincerity; and as she quickly perceived that it was utterly destitute of that tender interest and deep regard for the object beloved—a disposition which constitutes the essence of real love, the attentions of Sir Reginald became displeasing, and even disgusting. Agreeably to these her feelings, she, with dignified calmness, desired him, if his passion were indeed sincere, to combat and subdue a love so hopeless. Her representations to this effect were frequent, but seemingly ineffectual. She became, at length, uneasy and disturbed. She had urged his departure, as far as politeness would allow; yet he was still her guest.

She frequently confined herself, under various pretences, to her own apartment; thus obliging him to dine in the hall, with no other company than her own

domestics.

domestics. All this, however, was without effect. He assumed a consequence in her absence, which ill became a visitor; and he converted her absences into a proof of his own gallantry and attachment; declaring the days of attendance were well compensated, by a single sight of an object so beloved.

It was during Sir Reginald Harcland's visit at the castle, which had been thus unseasonably protracted, that the mysterious music was first heard in the woods— a circumstance which contributed in some degree to abstract her thoughts from the subject of her present vexation and perplexity; though this event rendered her by no means insensible to the propriety of Sir Reginald's removal from the castle, and she resolved to hasten it.

Nothing could be more calculated to interest

interest the attention of the Baroness, than this phenomenon of the musician-; and the difficulty of discovery increased her eagerness to inform herself who or what it could be that thus haunted the woods. She issued fresh orders, and a larger reward than before was offered for the detection of this extraordinary person. No one, however, could be either seen or traced; the sounds were therefore conceived to be something supernatural. This idea became, at length, so general, that those who had formerly made exertions for his discovery now abandoned the search, protesting they would have nothing to do with a spirit, and except Motley, the clown, or, as he was usually called, the Baroness's Fool, who, agreeable to the custom of the times, formed a part of the establishment at the castle, no

one

one had courage to pass the wood after a certain hour in the evening, or would even approach within some distance of it, without apprehension, and even terror, from the supposition of its being haunted. Even Father Osborne, the Baroness's confessor, the prior of an adjacent convent, was observed to seek another path, the direct one from the monastery leading along the side of the wood, and to cross himself, if, by chance being delayed somewhat later than usual at the castle, he caught the sounds of the mysterious music.

The Baroness's astonishment every day increased. Her mind was continually engaged and harrassed by the subject which now , perpetually engrossed her thoughts; it was at once pleasing and painful to her soul; alternately it elevated

vated her mind to enthusiasm, and sunk it into the depths of tender grief. She often spent whole hours alone in her oriel. Sometimes she would sit, as if engaged in a rumination so profound, as to absorb every faculty of her soul—sometimes gazing upon the tops of the woods that covered the heights around the castle, and, in one quarter, came almost close to the outer ditch, her eye, as it endeavoured to pierce their gloomy masses of shade, vainly attempting to descry some form which she might imagine to be that of the mysterious minstrel; then seizing her lute, she would strike, for a moment or two, the chords, then throw it from her, as though every note was discord which vibrated not from the strings of that instrument which had so greatly charmed her, that it seemed to have ob-

c 5   tained

tained the power of witchery over her senses.

When alone with Winifred, her companion and confidential woman, the course of her conversation could rarely be diverted to any other channel. Winifred, who could not but perceive the strong impression which had been made upon the mind of the Baroness by this really extraordinary circumstance, endeavoured to rouse her from the melancholy which seemed to be stealing upon her, and which was becoming every day more and more perceptible.

The alteration which had taken place in her Ladyship's habit and manners, would probably have occasioned Winifred much anxiety, though the cause was not unknown to her, had not her thoughts been occupied by other subjects, by which her

own

own mind was as thoroughly engrossed as was that of the Baroness. Sir Reginald Harcland, by his condescension, his flattery, his promises, and his presents, in all of which, since his arrival at the castle, he had been wonderfully profuse, had so ingratiated himself into the affections of Winifred, that she had been extremely anxious for the success of his suit, and had all along spoke of him to the Baroness in terms of the highest applause and commendation; never omitting any opportunity that offered of representing, in the most glowing colours, the distress in which the entire rejection of his addresses would involve the object of her cruelty; repeatedly declaring, that were she Sir Reginald, she would never relinquish the pursuit while life remained, but endeavour, by a constant course of attention and per-

c 6 severance,

severance, to obtain a return of that affection which, while thus unpitied and disregarded, formed his present misery, and might ultimately prove his ruin, and even death. Yet though Winifred had discovered in many instances that she had acquired an extraordinary influence over her Lady, an influence of which she was extremely vain, and which she always sought occasion to secure and increase, she never could so far deceive the Baroness, as to oblige her to view him with the same impartiality and admiration with which she herself regarded him; and failing in this attempt, her vexation was at least as great as her disappointment. Winifred had resided with the Baroness almost from her infancy. She had accompanied her, when she left the mansion of her father for the arms of an adoring husband,

husband, and was still her chief woman and attendant. It was on the bosom of Winifred that the Baroness sunk in speechless agony, on the news of the Baron's death; and that love of retirement which the Baroness thenceforth encouraged, contributed to render Winifred still more the object of her regard, by confiding, in converse with her, those sorrows in which she took so much pleasure to indulge.

In consequence of these feelings, and these habits of the Baroness, almost all offices of importance became delegated to Winifred, and she maintained an authority at the castle, which all envied and obeyed. Winifred, who, to an understanding by no means contemptible, united much art and cunning, found herself, by this arrangement, invested with almost

almost as much authority as the Baroness herself; and she perceived with the greatest satisfaction, that her interest and intervention were diligently solicited by every petitioner for any favour or benefit; and thus, not only in the internal concerns of the castle, but over the vassals and tenantry of the estates of the late Baron, her power was as absolute as her disposition was arbitrary.

The only persons at all likely to interrupt her views, or share her authority, were Genlinson, the Baron's steward, whose long series of fidelity had been gratefully acknowledged, and Motley, the clown, with whom the Baroness sometimes diverted herself, partly on account of his good sense as well as humour, but rather because he had been the favourite and occasional companion of her late lord.

From

From the uneasy fears and vexations excited by the former, from the favourable disposition of the Baroness towards her faithful domestic, Winifred was soon, as she conceived, happily relieved. The good old steward, who had grown grey in the service of the Lords of Fitzwalter, died a few months after the death of the Baron, of a disorder brought on, as was supposed, by grief for the loss of his beloved master. He was succeeded in his employment by a person appointed by Winifred, a Scotchman of the name of Maclawney, a man who, though he possessed a sufficient share of cunning to deceive the Baroness with a shew of honour and honesty, was every way unworthy of the trust reposed in him, his time being chiefly spent in idleness and debauchery. His chief, and indeed only aim,

aim, was to render himself agreeable to Winifred, an attempt in which he was by no means unsuccessful, Dame Winifred, as she was always called, being herself greatly averse to that species of cruelty she had all along reproved in the conduct of her Lady, and every way inclined to receive the assiduities of a lover, who, besides the advantage of being several years younger than herself, had the means in his power of acquiring riches and emoluments in which she some time hoped to share.

Amongst a train of inferior domestics, was a beautiful girl, called Ethelind, an humble attendant on Winifred. This maiden was the daughter of a mountain cottager, dwelling in the woody heights above the castle. Her mother had died when she was only six years of age; her father

father married again, though not till some
years after the death of his wife, a woman
by whom Ethelind was treated with so
much rigour and cruelty, that she obtained the kindest interest and compassion from all who knew her. She long
bore with patience a series of the severest
ill usage; but at length her father died,
and the situation of the poor girl became
most pitiable. The report of her ill treatment reached the ears of the Baroness,
who, after severely reprimanding the step-
mother for her cruelty to a poor unfortunate little orphan, thus left to her care,
received her into the castle.

Here Ethelind, who, at the period we
mention, was not quite fourteen years of
age, might have passed a life of ease and
happiness, had not Winifred's apprehensions suggested, that if suffered to be
much

much about the Baroness, she might supplant her in her affections, and put her upon devising means to estrange her from her Lady, her only friend and benefactress, a circumstance which served to render her situation, if not so irksome as before, exposed to many trials and inquietudes.

The Baroness, pleased with her beauty, had at first dressed her in a style superior to that of a common domestic. Her voice was extremely harmonious, and she had desired she should have some instruction in music. She was taught also needle-work and embroidery; and succeeded so well in every thing she undertook, that the Baroness was at once pleased and gratified.

Winifred perceived, with a jealousy which was every instant increasing, the partiality of the Baroness toward her new charge,

charge, and she eagerly sought occasion to ruin her in her esteem; and no artifices were unemployed, by which this scheme, however cruel and detestable, might be accomplished. She was accused of various misdemeanors, which at first, as they were only of a trifling nature, were but little noticed by the Baroness; but as these were continually multiplying, and the poor girl, when accused by Winifred before her Lady, dared not utter a single word in her defence, she began by degrees to abate in that confidence and regard she had at first entertained for her; and instead of being allowed, as formerly, to sit in her Lady's room, and await her orders, the unfortunate Ethelind was now, through the machinations of an envious favourite, usually confined to an apartment near the servants' hall, called Dame Winifred's

room,

room, where, except by stealth, none of
the domestics were allowed to visit her,
and where she usually sat at work till very
late in the evening; unless, as was now
and then the case, Mrs. Winifred recol-
lected some little matter wanted at the
castle, which might be had at a neighbouring village, when Ethelind, with a
wicker basket upon her arm, was dispatched to procure it.

These moments of liberty were, indeed, to Ethelind moments of delight;
for kept close to her work, and severely
tasked by Winifred, to be abroad and unrestrained, seemed the height of enjoyment. The plain, and somewhat unbe-
coming dress, which Winifred had selected
for her, in exchange for that she had first
worn, which she had observed to her Lady
had been the cause of her becoming extremely

tremely vain and forward, could neither hide the charms of her face, or the natural graces of her figure. Her fine long light hair, as if scorning the restraint of her hat, fell in many a vagrant tress on a bosom of transparent whiteness. Her soft blue eyes beamed with sensibility; her cheeks wore the blushes of the rose; her lips were tainted with vermilion, and when she spoke or smiled, displayed a sweetness of expression, which hardly painting can reach.

Nothing could exceed Ethelind's delight, when she had Dame Winifred's permission to go on an errand into the village, where she was sure to find something to amuse and interest her. These indulgences were however rare. The moments of liberty and enjoyment soon flitted away, while those of employment,

sometimes

sometimes difficult, and always irksome, which succeeded, were at once regular and unvaried.

Another object of Winifred's tyranny, was a young man, of the name of Edgar, the son of one of the Baroness's vassals, who, though not an inhabitant, was yet a frequent inmate at the castle: from his extreme vivacity when a boy, he had acquired the character of being wild; this his vivacity, however, never led him into any considerable faults; and as he advanced toward manhood, it became so tempered with prudence, that it was never suffered to proceed beyond the bounds of decorum; and as he wrote a fair hand, and understood arithmetic, even better than the steward, he was often employed to assist Mr. Maclawney in the writing out of his accounts, who, as his head was

seldom

seldom very clear, soon found him very useful, and even necessary to his occasions.

Dame Winifred, though she seldom condescended to converse with the humble Edgar, suffered his attendance; taking care, however, that Ethelind should not be present, lest, as she often observed, he should fill her head with vagaries, by telling the chit she was handsome. Edgar, who had been in habits of visiting at the castle when Ethelind was first admitted, when as children they had played together, had long, unknown to Dame Winifred, cherished a secret regard for the little orphan, which was now, as he had reached his eighteenth year, converted into a strong and tender interest.

Ethelind, thus designedly separated from the companion of her youth, seldom see-

ing

ing him, could not view him, when accident threw him in her way, without emotions of delight Edgar, ever upon the watch, let no opportunity escape of seeing or speaking to her: one day, suddenly entering the castle, and seeing the door of the apartment open in which she usually sat, he ventured to approach, and finding Ethelind alone, and in tears, entered the room. He eagerly and tenderly enquired what had happened to distress her, and vented so many reproaches upon those who could be the cause of such uneasiness, that Ethelind, whose distress was now converted into alarm, entreated he would leave her; nor could he for some time inform himself of the cause of her tears, till having pressed the subject again and again, he was informed that she had been severely treated by Dame Winifred

fred, for having, as she said, spoiled a bunch of flowers, she was working in a set of chairs, designed for her Lady s dressing-room, which she had done and undone several times with so little success, that Dame Winifred had declared they were every time worse than before; and had repeatedly assured her she should not be suffered to leave her work, even to go to bed, till she had finished it to her satisfaction.

Edgar, who was astonished at the beauty and elegance of the flowers, and the natural and graceful manner in which they were disposed, and who was utterly unable to behold the innocent Ethelind in tears, without experiencing the most affectionate and lively interest in her distresses, could not, on an avowal of the cause, restrain his indignation; and in

D   the

the expression of it, let fall some epithets, not very respectful toward Dame Wini- fred, who, accidentally hearing Edgar as he entered the room in which Ethelind was sitting, concealed herself behind the arras, so as to be unfortunately near enough to overhear the greater part of their discourse. No sooner did her ear catch the sound of these disdainful, and, as she conceived, highly insulting names, than she bounced from her concealment, and vented alike upon the innocent and guilty, the reproaches of a resentment too powerful to be either concealed or sup- pressed.

The consequence of this unlucky inci- dent was an encreased severity towards Ethelind, and the discharge of Edgar, who was commanded never more to enter the walls of the castle—a sentence which, however,

however, obtained some mitigation, from the interference of Maclawney, the steward, though owing to the watchful policy of Winifred, he could scarcely ever obtain a sight of his beloved Ethelind, who was more strictly confined, and more maliciously treated than ever.

CHAP

―――――――

CHAP. IV.

A Fool, a Fool!―――I met a Fool i' th' Forest,
A motley Fool, a miserable varlet:
As I do live by food, I met a Fool.

SHAKESPEARE.

FROM the relation of those events which preceded the era at which our history commences, we now return to the Baroness, in whose mind curiosity and astonishment surmounted every other feeling and reflection; and who, notwithstanding the various unsuccessful attempts which had been already made to discover the author of the mysterious minstrelsy, which was still heard nightly in the wood,

wood, was not less eager in her enquiries, or less profuse in her offers, to those who should have courage to pursue the sound, and trace the musician, if indeed mortal, to his asylum or hiding-place.

Day after day, and night after night, passed on, and no discovery was made; the clown had indeed been seen in the wood, but, except the clown, no one dared enter it; and from him nothing could be learnt, as he seldom gave a direct answer to any question, however important; and so little was there of method in every thing he said or did, that he was scarcely considered as rational.

The Baroness, who had heard that the clown had been seen returning from the wood at a late hour in the evening, and that he alone of all the domestics had

D 3   dared

dared to visit it about the minstrel hour,
summoned him into her presence.

"I sent for thee, Motley," said she,
"to enquire of thee, why thou goest into
that wood?"

"Marry, Lady," returned the clown,
"because no one else will."

"Does this afford any reason for thy
going thither?" resumed the Baroness.

"The best I know," answered the
clown, "and the best a man knows, is
the best he can give. But reason, which
is a quality of the brain, appertaineth not
unto fools. You call me fool, yet demand
from me that which fools have not.
What I have I can give, but what I have
not I cannot give; I cannot give thee
my reason, because being myself a fool,
ergo without reason, I have it not to be-
stow.

stow. So, Lady, if thou trustest to me for reason, thou must lack reason, and lacking it, become thyself little better than a true fool."

" Thou art a merry fellow," cried the Baroness, " nevertheless, being licensed to say any thing, art apt to grow impertinent. Were I less inclined to melancholy, I could be much diverted with thy jests. But in having first said thou hadst a reason, thou hast either spoiled thine own argument, or proved thou art no fool "

" Verily then should I prove myself a vagabond."

" How so?"

" Why, do I not live by my fooleries, and losing the capacity of foolishness, wouldst thou not take from me my coat, and reduce me to a level with those, who

D 4 having

having not that capacity, are obliged to practise from necessity upon those that have ?"

" I would gladly have thee lose this capacity, as thou callest it," cried the Baroness, " were it only for a moment. Prithee, good fool, step out of thy fooleries, and answer me one simple question—why dost thou go into that wood ?"

" Marry, for the same reason that I would not go to court."

" What is that ?"

" Because there I meet no bad company."

" It were a better reason, hadst thou said thou wentest thither to meet good company—But to the purpose Hast thou, Motley, I mean after evening, when the mantle of night is spread abroad,

and

and begins to embrown with horror the shades of you drear wood, seen aught in it beside thyself?"

"Thou questionest deeply, Lady," cried the clown. "Yea, I have seen the toad and the adder, the bat, the owl, and the fox."

"I speak not of the beasts and reptiles of the earth," resumed the Baroness. "I ask thee, Motley, whether, in thy nightly wanderings through the wood, thou hast seen any human being, or any thing bearing a resemblance to the human form?'

"Truly," quoth the clown, "I have seen something."

"When?"

"Last night."

"Where—where, good Motley?"

"Within the pale of the wood"

"Indeed! what was it?"

"A fair

" A fair and noble figure, of a sweet and delicate proportion The moon shone bright. I advanced, it preceded me; I turned, it turned also; I bowed, it bowed; I started, it started; it observed, and copied my every motion."

" Thou hast then, indeed, seen something; speak—speak, good Motley; what was it that thou sawest? was it a human being, or———"

" It was not a human being," interrupted Motley, " but the shadow or representation of one; having in itself no substance, though a form."

" This answers to a spirit," cried the Baroness. " Of what size was it?"

" About my size, Lady; yet, methinks, upon recollection, it appeared somewhat taller."

" Bore it any instrument of music?"

" No,

" No, Lady, none."

" Spirits are said to have the power of assuming various shapes and forms: how did it appear to you?"

" In the most pleasing one."

" Describe it, good Motley."

" The moon described it most aptly, I mean the outline; for lacking colours, the moon is but an indifferent painter."

" What did it represent?"

" In the first place, two legs of the most excellent symmetry; a body, with arms correspondingly graceful; a head erect, surmounted and adorned with a cap and bells, singularly ornamented."

" I'll be sworn, fool," cried the Baroness, " thou art describing thine own shadow. Enough of this fooling—speak instantly, and to the purpose, or I will have thee beat for thy ill-timed jestings.

Sawest

Sawest thou aught in the wood besides thyself, and the representation of thyself in thine shadow?"

"Yes, Lady, I saw——"

"What didst thou see?"

"Two turtle doves in a nest. They were cooing together, and seemed happy. The old mate of the female bird returned, as it seemed after a long absence, and found its nest pre-occupied by a stranger: it moaned, and went apart. I heard its melancholy cooings, from a tree at some distance from whence I stood. It seemed not to have even entered the nest; but sought to hide itself and its griefs, even from those that had caused it."

"Alas, poor, pretty bird!" cried the Baroness. "Then thou hast seen nothing, Motley; yet that wood, they say, is haunted, and under such circumstances,

methinks

methinks thy courag e m ɩ ꞁ ꞁ ꞁ ꞁ ꞁ ꞁ ꞁ
to have entered it. Thou hast heard the
mysterious music, fool, and yet thou art
undaunted. Shouldst thou fear, Motley,
wert thou to see a spirit?"

"I have seen many, Lady; but I would
not willingly see one without its case."

"True, disembodied, and apart from
its earthly tenement, the mind recoils
at it."

"But as the spirit," resumed Motley,
"has never yet appeared in any shape
but the shape of the sound of the lute,
played by the picture of nobody——"

"Thou hast yet courage to visit its.
haunts," cried the Baroness.

"Truly, Lady, courage is a good quality, and, being a good quality, I would
not wear it out: yet not to use it, would
be

be to make it fall into disuse, and thereby become rusty, and unfit for service."

"Thou art a wise fellow, after all," cried the Baroness. "Here, take this money, visit nightly the wood, and shouldst thou bring with thee any intelligence which may lead to a discovery of this incident, thy diligence shall be rewarded."

"I will receive thy money, Lady; but although I should not lack wisdom to assist thee, take not from me, I beseech thee, my prerogative of foolishness. Adieu, fair Lady, adieu; may the god of mirth dispossess you of your present melancholy, and make you merry as the cricket; and as wise too; for the cricket slinks into his hole, when attempted to be caught by the hand of impertinence."

Clown

Clown sings.

From those eyes, on beds of roses,
Let not sweet the tear-drop flow;
Time oft wond'rous things discloses,
Stem, oh stem, this tide of woe.

" Pretty words, and very well sung,"
cried the Baroness; " where didst thou
learn that stanza?"

" I learnt it of the god of love, who
bade me address it to thy most excellent
beauty."

" Away—away," said the Baroness,
" thou flatterest: take thy money and
begone."

CHAP.

CHAP. V.

Lieve arboscel cui debil aura siede,
Lieve augellin che geme o che si move,
Lieve foglia che cade o che si scote,
Di terror doppia il dubbia cor percote.

ARIOSTO.

THE clown had departed, and the Baroness had nearly fallen into one of her
accustomed fits of melancholy musing,
when her attention was engaged by the
entrance of Winifred, who had brought a
letter for the Baroness. On opening it,
she discovered it to be from Lord Broke
her father, the friend and highly esteemed
courtier

courtier of Henry the Seventh. She received it with satisfaction and delight;
but ere she had perused the contents, her
lips trembled, her cheeks grew pale, and
had not a plentiful shower of tears come
at that instant to her relief, she would
have fainted in the arms of her attendant.

"Oh Winifred!" exclaimed she, at
length recovering herself, "I am the
most wretched of human beings."

"Fresh troubles—alack, alack!" interrupted Winifred, "what has happened,
Lady? sure the Lord Fitzwalter——"

"To-morrow," resumed the Baroness,
"the Earl of Ormond, a nobleman of the
first rank and power, arrives at the castle."

"Well, Lady, and what of that?"

"He is sent hither," continued the
Baroness, "by the king, and comes
bearing the royal authority; by which, as
a ward

a ward of state, I may be consigned by marriage, to take possession of me and my domains.   Lord Broke, my father, is to accompany him. Oh that I were some simple maiden, such as Ethelind, unincumbered by castles and domains, and therefore an object of state caution ; for then I might follow my inclinations, for no one would seek my hand, and I might mourn my lost husband with uninterrupted sorrow."

" Ah, Lady," cried Winifred, " greatness is indeed, a plague."

" And yet," continued the Baroness, " perhaps he may not wish to wed a melancholy mope like me; and from what I learn by this letter, he is of too noble a nature, to submit his inclinations in this particular, even to a monarch's will, and I may escape his nuptials."

" Why,

" Why, my Lady, methinks you must
not build too much upon that," cried
Winifred; " he will not reject you and
your domains too. But he has then, it
seems, the power of rejecting you, whilst
you, Lady, are denied the privilege of
refusing him, however disagreeable he may
prove."

" Such, if I understand it, is the im
port of this letter," resumed the Baroness.
" So runs my destiny."

" Would to Heaven you had escaped it
by marrying Sir Reginald !" exclaimed
Winifred.

" My situation would then have been
even more intolerable," said the Baroness,
" than as the wife of the Earl of Ormond.
This Lord, they say, is noble; but how
great soever his merits and deserts, it will
be to me the greatest misfortune, and to
my

my feelings the most distressing, to receive him, or any one, for a husband.
Indeed, Winifred, my heart dwells with
the fondest delight on the memory of its
first attachment, and the thought is to me
most disgusting, which suggests the possibility of my receiving another lord."

"Oh, Lady! were you less handsome,
and less powerful."

"Would to Heaven," cried the Baroness, "I were the most deformed of the
human species, so I might escape my present embarrassments!"

"Suppose," said Winifred, "you were
to invent some disguise, or use something
which might discolour and conceal the
beauty of your face. I have heard that
weeds, and the juices of some flowers,
applied to the skin, will so change the
complexion of it, as to turn fairness into
deformity:

deformity: what if we were to procure these juices?"

"I would not be averse from any innocent stratagem," replied the Baroness, "by which the dearest purpose of my heart, that of being allowed to remain in my present state of widowhood, might be secured to me; but should the Earl be, as he is represented in this letter, a man of peerless virtue and knightly honour, would it not be better to throw myself upon his generosity, by an avowal of my real sentiments respecting him, and a declaration of the decided aversion I do and always shall entertain, against a second union, and try to induce him to persuade the king not to insist upon my second marriage?"

"Ah, Lady, but if this should fail?"

"If it should, his character has been misrepresented;

misrepresented; he cannot in that case be
a man of honour: I will try, however,
this scheme; I will at least make the
attempt; should it not succeed, I have, I
think, yet another resource, in the tenderness of a beloved and highly-revered
father, whose influence at court, if properly exerted in the cause of his unhappy
daughter, may save me from a grievance
so full of evil."

"Well, Lady, with these hopes you will
then consent to see the Earl."

"I must see him," returned the Baroness, "and he must be received with the
honours due to his rank and character.
His appearance here will be favourable to
me in one respect; Sir Reginald Harcland,
who must have been already impatient of
my frequent absences from him, must
now, in common decency, depart; let him

be

be informed immediately of the intended arrival of Earl Ormond; and further, that it is my pleasure he should not await that event."

"Alas—alas!" cried Winifred, sighing heavily, "I would fain not be the messenger of such heart-breaking tidings."

"Go this instant," said the Baroness, "and convey this my message to the knight. Tell him, as the near kinsman of my Lord, I greeted him well, but that I now expect his departure."

Winifred frowned, but was retiring.

"Stop, Winifred," cried the Baroness; "tell him not the name of the guest whose arrival here we expect to-morrow. Say only it is a nobleman sent hither by the king. He will guess the motive of his coming hither; if not, you may be more explicit. Plead your ignorance as to his

his name, lest, in the heat of his indignation, he should drop some expressions
of an affronting nature, concerning this
Earl, before my people, which may afterwards be repeated to his attendants, and
thus reach the ear of their Lord. The
knight is rash and impetuous; and we
cannot be too circumspect, and hardly
sufficiently cautious, in our endeavours
to hinder any quarrel which might arise
from such imprudence, between two
nobles, both, perhaps, highly tenacious,
and equally scrupulous, in respect to
points of honour."

Winifred withdrew, and the Baroness
retired to her oriel, where, seated, she
marked the dewy-fingered night con-
tending with the summer twilight, which
refused to yield to her wonted sway. The
lake spread its placid bosom full in view,
and

and no sound, save the sleepy twitter of the martlet from its earth-made nest in the fretwork of the parapet, varied the stillness of the hour. "This scene," cried the Baroness, "invites to tranquillity, at least till morning. Be hushed, my alarms and anxieties, I will not——"

At this instant the minstrel of the woods began his minstrelsy. "Oh Heavens!" exclaimed the Baroness, and again stood wrapt in listening astonishment. The music gradually approached; it swelled louder and louder: meanwhile the moon rose cloudless in the eastern sky, and threw its silvery gleam upon the rocks and ivy-crusted turrets of the castle; a thousand stars gemmed the heavens, and all seemed attention to the mysterious minstrel, when

E   At

" At last a sweet and solemn breathing sound
Rose like a steam of rich distill'd perfumes,
And stole upon the air, that even SILENCE
Was took ere she was 'ware, and wish'd she might
Deny her nature, and be never more,
Still to be thus displaced."

At this time there was something in the tones of the music, even more affecting than usual. It was of a dirge-like sadness, yet so soft, so dulcet, that as the Baroness continued to listen, tears streamed involuntarily from her eyes. It now somewhat varied the measure, and she thinking, perhaps it might be the guardian spirit of her deceased Lord, to whom she conceived every sound bore some tender import, perhaps gently reproving her for her want of fidelity in receiving new suitors in his castle, or rather, as it seemed, warning her against some coming danger, seconded with

9   thoughts

thoughts like these, the sounds seemed to have obtained a talismanic power over the bewildered senses of the Baroness. They overpowered her feelings; a sudden faintness came over her. " Great Heaven!" exclaimed she in transport; and she sunk almost fainting against the arras. Ere she had time to recollect her scattered senses, and question the reality of what she had heard, the music ceased—it was heard no more.

The Baroness, trembling with an agitation which almost deprived her of the power of motion, retired to her room, and soon afterwards to her bed; but sleep forsook her pillow, and she arose on the eventful day, which was to introduce her to Earl Ormond, and dismiss Sir Reginald from the castle, without having once tasted the blessing of repose.

E 2   CHAP.

―――――――

CHAP. VI.

Learn, cruel! learn, that this afflicted heart,
This heart which Heav'n delights to prove with tortures,
Did it not love, has power and pride to shun you.

ZARA.

SIR Reginald, on receiving the above
message from the Baroness, which, though
conveyed as a request, was, in effect, an
order for him to quit the castle without
delay, and especially on hearing that another suitor was expected, broke out into
all the extravagances of the most violent
frenzy. He positively refused to depart,
without first seeing the Baroness. He
even

even threatened to arm his vassals, and lay waste her domains, unless this was granted him. This his determination he sent the Baroness, who, uneasy at his violence, returned excuses.

He declared, on receiving these, he would assault her castle, in revenge for the insult of an abrupt dismission.. Although the Baroness was sensible she might rely for defence on the fidelity of her dependants, and was sure of redress, from the influence of her father at court, yet she thought it might be prudent to bend a little, to prevent evil consequences; and she agreed to receive him in the hall, surrounded by her retinue. To this he could not object, although he would have wished for privacy; and he returned a message of thanks to the Baroness for the honour she conceded him.

E 3

The

The Baroness immediately gave orders for his audience in form, which she intimated was intended as an honour due to a visitor and a kinsman, about to take his leave.

A chair of state, raised by a step in front, was placed on the upper platform of the grand hall, where the family dined on public occasions; and before it were spread carpets of tissued tapestry. The seneschal, at the head of twenty halberdiers, occupied two stations, one on the right, the other on the left, immediately below the platform; and all the higher servants, and such of the Baroness's vassals as the suddenness of the business could allow, were arranged in two lines below them. Behind the chair stood several of the inmates of the castle, who were either distantly related to the family,

and

and were, on that account, allowed a constant table, or else were the sons of gentry connected with the family, and retained to serve as pages, and receive, in return, instruction and exercise in all those arts and accomplishments which suited the character of the knight or the courtier. At the doors were stationed parties of the yeomen of the guard, supported by the servants of the buttery and kitchen, habited in their best liveries, and bearing staves. The porter and his whifflers, clad also in their liveries of state, took their stations at the gates and various entries; and rows of archers and arquebusiers in the court, formed a sort of line of approach toward the flight of steps leading to the great hall.

All things being thus arranged, Sir Reginald, followed by the groom of his

chamber,

chamber, was conducted to audience by the steward and two mace-bearers; and presently the Baroness entered from a side door, attended by Winifred and the maidens of her chamber, and seating herself on the prepared seat, received Sir Reginald with that state and dignity which the Barons Fitzwalter always observed on important occasions, in common with others of the same rank with themselves in the realm.

Sir Reginald, piqued by all these formalities, which he was sensible boded him no good, appeared with a haughty demeanor and proud look, seeming to acknowledge these attentions to be his due, although he was ready to receive them with scorn. The conflict of various passions, which reigned within him, was evidently great. Love and wounded pride seemed

seemed to be struggling for pre-eminence, as he approached the chair on which the Baroness was seated.

The Baroness perceived, and was uneasy at these emotions; and apprehensive lest the warmth of his passion should hurry him into expressions which might be wounding to her delicacy, resolved to hasten the conclusion of an interview, which exposed those feelings to the observation of so many witnesses. From motives, therefore, of the most delicate consideration of the situation of Sir Reginald, as well as that of herself, she addressed him in a speech appropriate to the occasion, in which she acknowledged the high opinion she had conceived of him, and the strong sense she entertained of the honour he had designed to confer upon her, in his late proposals of mar-

E 5   riage;

riage; an honour for which she assured
him she was not less grateful than if she
had consented to accept it. Then hastening to take her leave, she added, with
great sweetness, "Farewell, Sir Knight,
farewell; commend me to your honourable
family; and be assured, though I cannot,
under the present circumstances of my
situation, invite your longer continuance
in my castle, it will always afford me
pleasure to hear of your welfare."

Then, as if anxious to prevent affording
him any opportunity of reply, she arose,
courteously bowing, and was retiring.
Sir Reginald, little expecting that the
audience he had so urgently requested
was to terminate thus abruptly, would
have remonstrated, and led the Baroness
back to her seat; but she refused to be
reconducted thither; and mildly observing
she

she had nothing further to add, withdrew, attended by her women, through
the door by which she had entered;
leaving Sir Reginald, notwithstanding the
politeness of her address, and the manner
in which she had expressed her sentiments
concerning him, overcome with vexation
and disappointment.

CHAP.

CHAP. VII.

——— 'Twas but a dream:

But then so terrible, it shakes my soul,

Cold drops of dew hang on my trembling flesh———

My blood grows chilly, and I freeze with horror!

SHAKESPEARE.

THE Baroness, after having waited about
an hour, anxiously expecting the departure of Sir Reginald, was informed, at
length, that the knight, having relapsed
into one of his accustomed fits of distraction and vehemence, had positively refused to quit the castle, unless the Baroness should first grant him another interview,

view, which he now insisted should be a private one. This his declaration and resolve was conveyed to the Baroness by Winifred, who warmly interceded for her Lady's consent to the Knight's request, as she called it, though from the authoritative terms in which it was dictated, it seemed rather to take the nature of a command.

" Oh my Lady !" said Winifred, "you must indeed see him once again; you know not what may be the consequence of a refusal."

" I have, indeed, every thing to apprehend from his violence," replied the Baroness; " why will he not remain satisfied with my determination, and what I have already granted? he must, ere this, have known that my resolution is not to be shaken

shaken by any arts or arguments he can use."

" Ah, Lady! but when he loves so tenderly, and mourns so grievously! Had you but seen him last night—Oh, never shall I forget him!"

" Last night!" repeated the Baroness.

" Ah, Lady! long after I took your message, cruelly desiring him to leave the castle this morning, in the middle of the night, I had no sleep myself, not a wink, for I could think of nothing but Sir Reginald; it was a stormy and very dreadful night; the wind blew loud, and the rain beat hard against the windows, and the owls, from the turrets, screamed so dismally, that——

" The wind was indeed tempestuous," interrupted the Baroness; " but what had the

the storm of the night to do with Sir Reginald?"

"You shall hear, Lady," answered Winifred. "The wind, as I was saying, howled dismally, and, as it rushed through the galleries, made such strange noises, for I suppose it was nothing but the wind, which, you know, often makes sudden squalls through the passages, that I began, I don't know how, to be strangely terrified, and so I got up: you, Lady, was asleep, I think, though as I made but little noise, and the wind continued very boisterous, you might not, perhaps, hear me, even if you were awake. Just as I opened my door, I saw Sir Reginald darting out of his chamber, pale as ashes, with a lamp in his hand, and nothing on but a long loose gown, which reached nearly to his feet; I asked him what was the

the matter, and where he was going. At
first I thought he might be walking in
his sleep; but I soon found he was as
wide awake as I was.

'Winifred,' said he, with a look of
terror and amazement, 'have you seen
any thing to-night?'—'Seen any thing, Sir
Knight,' said I, 'what should I see? I
am not superstitious, for all this spirit in
the wood, as it never comes into the
castle, and keeps, as one may say, at a
proper distance, and I hope you are not.
Why, surely, you do not think you have
seen any thing, do you?'—'I don't know,
Winifred,' said he: 'but did you hear
nothing?'—'I heard nothing,' said I, 'but
the wind, and the dismal hooting of the
owls from the buildings. But where are
you going, Sir Knight?' said I, 'and why
are you so frightened?'—'I have had a
strange

strange dream, Winifred,' said he, ' if it was a dream.'—' A dream!' said I, ' la! I often dream dismal things myself, and they terrify me for a time; but when the light of the morning comes, these frightful fancies disperse, and I think no more about them—no more will you; so, pray, Sir Knight, go back to your chamber, lie down in bed, and try to get a little sound sleep.'—' The light of the morning will not, I fear, dispel the dismal images of the night,' cried Sir Reginald; ' but I will take your advice, Winifred, and endeavour——Oh, Winifred, if it were not for your lovely Lady's cruelty!' Then he sighed deeply, and entered his chamber; and I heard him pacing about the room for some time. When I thought he was in bed, I returned to my own apartment, but I could not sleep; for his

griefs.

griefs and sufferings, which I really
thought had affected his head, had so
disturbed my mind, that I could not com-
pose myself to rest. Oh, my Lady! you
must, indeed, you must see him. He
says, if you will grant him one interview
in private, or with only me being present,
he will leave the castle immediately."

"Says he this," cried the Baroness,
" and, upon the honour of a knight, may
I believe him? if so, upon these conditions, I consent once more to see him.
Go, tell him this, and that in your presence I will instantly give him audience.

Winifred withdrew with this message
from the Baroness, and shortly afterwards
Sir Reginald entered the Baroness's anti-
room, where she usually received her
guests. She was reclining upon a crimson velvet settee, superbly ornamented
with

with gold, attended by Winifred, when Sir Reginald approached. She arose on seeing him, and accosted him with the same winning courtesy of address which she always observed in her salutations Sir Reginald, notwithstanding the permission granted to his request, entered with an air of wildness and distraction, that greatly alarmed the Baroness. He seemed to be struggling to speak, but could not; his eyes roved wildly over her figure; he leaned against the arras, and seemed, for a moment or two, to be utterly incapable of speech or motion.

"Give me not cause to repent, Sir Reginald," cried the Baroness mildly, yet with some emotion, her sweet eyes beaming softness and sensibility, "that I have thus, perhaps against my better judgment, in compliance with your importunities,

portunities, your very urgent solicitations, consented to grant you that audience you so earnestly desired before your departure from my castle. Till your avowal of the sentiments you entertain for me, which, for I have never in any instance deceived you, you well know not to be reciprocal, I considered and treated you as a friend and kinsman, the kinsman of my highly-revered and most tenderly-regretted husband. Had you not exceeded the bounds of that friendship and honourable esteem which you at first professed for me, and which, while it did not militate against my principles or my feelings, I scrupled not to return, my present command, which I again repeat, that you must immediately quit this place, would have been unnecessary. Could I have doubted the propriety of the measure I am

I am enforcing, your present behaviour, Sir Reginald, would have convinced me of its indispensibility. Let me then save you and myself the trouble of all further altercation on this subject—a subject which has been the occasion of much uneasiness and anxiety to both of us, by repeating my most earnest wishes for your future welfare and happiness, and pronouncing a farewell, which I now expect to be final."

"Heaven and earth!" exclaimed Sir Reginald, striking his forehead with vehemence, as if but newly awakened to a full sense and conviction of his present hopeless destiny, "is all then over?—am I doomed to be the most wretched, the most scorned of human beings?"

"You cannot long be wretched, Sir Reginald," resumed the Baroness, "but

by

by your own fault. Your merits and
your rank may readily secure you an
alliance with the most honourable families in England; and give you a spouse
more fair and worthy of you than the
cold affections of the widow of your
friend. Cease then to disgrace yourself
by these unworthy fits of vehemence, so
ill becoming a man of your rank; and
may the saints of Heaven give you
that happiness which your conduct will
then deserve!"

"How aptly can those reason," pursued Sir Reginald, "and apply balms and
remedies to the bursting breaking heart,
who have never felt the dart of anguish!"

"I would teach you, by my example,"
cried the Baroness, "that those who have
felt its keenest arrow, can prescribe cures
for

for the inflicted wound; we may suffer, but we ought not therefore to despair. You see before you, Sir Reginald, one who has had many sorrows, the widowed wife of Fitzwalter: you knew him well, I need not therefore expatiate upon his virtues; they are registered in the hearts of all that knew him. You are not unacquainted with his misfortunes: you know too how I revered, how I loved, how I adored!"

"And yet it is not for him I am rejected," cried Sir Reginald, accompanying this remark with a look of scrutinizing enquiry, and haughty vehemence. "No! the image of the departed Fitzwalter is supplanted in that heart, where late it held, you say, an undivided empire, though not by me."

"How!" exclaimed the Baroness.

"Time

" Time and your tears," resumed Sir Reginald, "have erazed and washed away the remembrance of him who was your husband; and bright, tearless, and beaming with renovated hope and promised joy, those eyes now seek another home than that which death has banished from them. Ormond comes forth to meet their willing glances—oh that, basilisk-like, there were death in them!—he comes, and is accepted."

"Ormond!" reiterated the Baroness—then recollecting her injunction to Winifred, she added, " My woman, I find, Sir Knight, has been more communicative on this subject than I expected; it were well had she paid more attention to my orders."

" What were those orders, Lady?"

" That she should convey a message, informing

informing you that a stranger, whose name I bade her conceal, was to arrive this day at the castle, and that I expected and desired your departure should precede the approach of the expected guest."

"Your words, Lady, are the very echoes of those conveyed to me by your woman."

"Ah! how then could you know?"

"By no human tongue," said Sir Reginald, "was I informed of the name and quality of the person whose arrival here is expected."

"By no human tongue!" repeated the Baroness; "you must then have had intelligence of it in writing: is it already so well known that the Earl of Ormond intends a visit at my castle?"

"Neither by letter, or verbally by any natural means," returned Sir Reginald,

F   "have

" have I been apprized of the Earl's intention, or the motive of his coming hither."

" Neither by a written account, or verbally by any natural means !' resumed the Baroness ; " your words are paradoxes, Sir Knight; how then could you obtain your information ?"

" Deem me not weakly superstitious, Lady, when I declare, I obtained it by means wholly supernatural—by a dream—"

" A dream, Sir Reginald !"

" By a dream or a vision, I know not whether one or the other, in which Baron Fitzwalter, your late husband, and my most dear friend, appeared to me !"

" Ah ! my husband !" exclaimed the Baroness, her hands raised, and clasped together in an attitude of astonishment.

" Did I not tell you, Lady," said Winifred,

nifred, " how Sir Reginald, last night, rushed from his chamber, pale as death, and trembling with agitation, as from some sudden fright, and how he questioned me, whether I had seen or heard any thing?"

" Was this the dream you spoke of?" cried the Baroness; " was this the cause of his alarm?"

" Methought I was awake," pursued Sir Reginald ; " yet it might be but a dream—a wild and fearful dream!"

"What was it? asked the Baroness, whose curiosity was now greatly excited.

" It were imprudent to reveal it, Lady ; the substance might alarm you."

" No matter, I must hear it," said the Baroness—" proceed."

" Do you command, Lady ?"

" I earnestly entreat to know its import—haste, and inform me of it."

F 2   " I would

" I would be excused."

" Nay, prithee let me hear it."

" It may disturb and terrify you much."

" Still let me know it—I beseech, command——"

" Well then, I *must* obey.—Last night," resumed Sir Reginald, " it seemed, not long after I had retired to my bed, the moon shining full into my chamber, I saw a figure resembling, nay, the exact representation, of the late Baron, moving slowly towards me. The door of the apartment was closed, and even locked, so that no one could have entered. I watched its motions, in silent astonishment; it walked, or rather glided, to my bed-side; the curtains seemed to move untouched; and while the beams of a cloudless moon fell upon its face——"

" Oh,

" Oh, Heavens!" exclaimed the Baroness.

" I saw every lineament—it was himself—it was Fitzwalter."

" And seemed it not to be a dream?" cried the Baroness, shuddering.

" It seemed to myself," said Sir Reginald, " as though I were as much awake as at this instant."

" Ah! and how did it appear to you?"

" In complete armour."

" How looked it?"

" Pale, and very sorrowful."

" Great Heaven!" exclaimed the Baroness, " yet it was *but a dream!*"

" And did the figure speak to you?" asked the Baroness.

" Yes; it was from this airy nothing— this unsubstantial form—this apparition,

that

that I learned of the purposed arrival of Earl Ormond."

"Amazing !" exclaimed the Baroness, "yet it was *but a dream:* and what said it of this Ormond ?"

"It spoke of him in terms of hatred, expressed, however, rather in respect to his family than himself, those of Ormond and Fitzwalter having been long at variance."

"Did any thing else seem to pass?" asked the Baroness impatiently.

"Yes: it declared the spirit of Fitzwalter could not rest, while the enemy of his family remained a guest at this castle; and that——"

"What else?"

"I have promised to divulge no more."

"Yet

" Yet speak," reiterated the Baroness;
" it was, you know, *but a dream.*"

" Were I fully assured of that," pursued Sir Reginald ; " but no, I have sworn "

" I pray you be explicit."

" I must be silent : but let me conjure you, as you value the repose of your once honoured Lord, let not Ormond lead you to the altar."

" What, in that case, would be the penalty ?"

" There, too, *I must be silent.* Urge me not, Lady—I have promised—nay, I have sworn."

" Said it aught else," cried the Baroness, " that, without a breach of promise and good faith, you might divulge?"

" Little, till parting; when, with a

look

look expressive more of sorrow than of anger, it breathed a wish——"

" Ah ! what was it?"

" That you had made a worthier choice than either Ormond's love or wi‑dowhood."

" Amazing ! what meant it then ?"

" It looked at me; and love, and sweet affection, beamed from its sunken eye. It was a noble, but a fearful sight."

" And most amazing !" pursued the Baroness;" " but, remember, Sir Knight, *it was but a dream;* and dreams are fashioned of the remnants of our waking thoughts. Said it, indeed, Lord Ormond would be here to night?"

" It did."

" This was most strange ! such predictions, when verified, savour of super‑natural

natural agency, even though conveyed in a dream. Lord Ormond, indeed, arrives to-night; and, as the day is wearing fast, I conjure you, Sir Reginald, to make our parting short."

" Yes, Lady," rejoined Sir Reginald, as if inspired with a sudden resolution, " *it shall be short*. Inexorable in your re-solves, I leave you to your fate. Adieu, Madam, adieu.

" Adieu, Sir Reginald," cried the Ba-roness faintly; then, as if fearful of en-creasing his uneasiness by a constrained coldness, she held out her hand, adding, " Though I cannot give you my love, be assured you possess my esteem; and never, till you shall have violated the laws of honour and decorum, will you lose it. May prosperity attend you throughout

your

your days, and every earthly felicity be yours !"

Sir Reginald seized the hand she presented, and carried it to his lips, faltered out something he could not express articulately, and then hastened from the room, and in the course of another hour, publicly left the castle.

CHAP.

―――――――――――

CHAP. VIII.

———— ———I cannot love him;
Yet I suppose him virtuous, know him noble,
Of great estate, of fresh and stainless youth ;
In voices well divulg'd ; free, learn'd, and valiant;·
And in dimension, and the shape of nature,
A gracious person ; but yet. I cannot love him.

SHAKESPEARE

THE Baroness ruminated upon the subject of this extraordinary dream, which,
in whatever way she contemplated it,
partook largely of the marvellous. Sir
Reginald had declared that he had not
been informed by Winifred, or any other
human means, of the expected arrival of

F 6   Earl

Earl Ormond. She had no reason to doubt his veracity; nor could she, even for a moment, imagine he would dare to impose upon her with a fiction. The image of the Baron had then certainly been represented to him in a dream, so like reality, as to leave him, even then, uncertain whether he had not indeed beheld his disembodied spirit. He had, in fancy, if not in reality, both seen and conversed with him. The conversation he had in part revealed, but bound, as it seemed, by a solemn engagement, to preserve an eternal silence respecting the rest, it remained involved in mystery and obscurity. When struck by an astonishing connection of incidents and events, rarely imaged in dreams, for the most part wild and disarranged, it appeared supernatural; and, while the possibility occurred

occurred to her that it might not be, as she had at first imagined, a mere chimera of the brain, in the absence of reason and reflection, but a real appearance, a shuddering sensation seized her, and the very blood seemed to chill in her veins.

With a view of obtaining a more thorough knowledge and satisfaction on the subject on which she had before questioned Sir Reginald, she addressed enquiries to Winifred, who, without the least hesitation or confusion, repeated the words she had delivered in her message to Sir Reginald; and thus, could a remaining doubt have lingered in her mind, it would now have been wholly dissipated: Winifred, who had been present at the interview between Sir Reginald and the Baroness, expressed an astonishment not

inferior

inferior to that which the Baroness herself felt.

Anxious, however, to calm the mind of
her Lady, which she perceived was greatly
agitated and disturbed, perhaps more than
she was herself aware of, she prudently
discouraged the idea, that what had been
thus forcibly pourtrayed to Sir Reginald's
fancy, whatever appearance of reality it
might assume, could be any thing but a
dream; and by the recollection and enu-
meration of various others of a like
nature, almost equally extraordinary, in
which persons, not unknown to her, had
seen, or seemed to have seen, their departed friends, she sought to divert the
thoughts of the Baroness from the subject of her present agitation and astonishment, and prepare her for an interview
with

with Earl Ormond, whose arrival was now
hourly expected. Lord Broke, who had
been dispatched by the King on an embassy to James the Third, who, at that
time, filled the throne of Scotland, was
to accompany him to the castle; but the
nature of his mission requiring expedition, and not admitting of delay, he
was to remain there only the night, and
to proceed early on the following day to
the Court of Scotland.

Never, perhaps, was there a period
when the Baroness could be less disposed
to meet the approach of an intended
suitor, the favourite of a King, whose
power over females of rank and estate,
according to the usages of the realm, was
even greater than that of a father, and
especially over her, as the widow of the
attainted Fitzwalter. One circumstance

5   afforded

afforded some consolation. Lord Broke would be present at the introduction of Ormond; and even should it be impossible for him to continue his stay at the castle, during the whole of the Earl's visit, she hoped to be able to win from him a promise to use his utmost efforts to prevent a marriage, which she could not think of without anguish, or even without abhorrence. So great, indeed, was her repugnance to every thought of this union, that she resolved, rather than become the wife of Earl Ormond, to dare the vengeance of the offended sovereign, stern and arbitrary as he was known to be; and, should he so far exert his prerogative, as to seize her fiefs, and confine her to the most remote and solitary monastery, to submit to any decree that might be passed against her, rather than sacrifice

her

her principles and feelings to the uncontrouled sway of kingly power.

Winifred, whose mind was not less busied by various plans than that of the Baroness, in endeavouring to suggest means to free her Lady from her present difficulties and embarrassments, warmly interested herself in her distresses; even those of Sir Reginald seemed forgotten; for Winifred, probably from a conviction that all she might urge, or say, in his cause, under the present unfavourable circumstances, would be ineffectual, forbore to mention even his name. All reasonable hopes of persuading the Baroness to this marriage were now at an end; and she yielded to what she really thought was necessity. She did not doubt, even for a moment, but that the Earl would be enamoured of the Baroness; and that however

however unsuccessful he might finally
prove in his attempts to gain her affections, he would, on no account, be persuaded to relinquish a prize, which, supported as were his pretensions by the
authority of the king, she but too easily
foresaw he had almost the power to command.

Her Lady's beauty, of which Winifred
had formerly been as vain as if she had herself possessed the lovely fleeting charm, she
now contemplated with dissatisfaction, and
even with regret; for she saw in it one of
the greatest obstacles to her own wishes,
and those of the Baroness; and happy,
at this moment, would she have been, if
possessing the wand of Urgando, she
could have metamorphosed beauty into
deformity. In vain she endeavoured to
select a dress, which might conceal or
detract

detract from the native graces of her Lady's figure. Art could neither effectually diminish, nor effectually encrease what nature had so liberally conferred; and she perceived, with regret, that the Baroness, when attired to wait the expected approach of Lord Ormond, appeared even more than usually brilliant and fascinating.

Whatever might be the beauty of the Baroness, it afforded her no pleasure or satisfaction; nay, her vigorous mind little regarded that, to her, worthless quality. Occupied by the most uneasy presages, she had dismissed her woman, and, meditating alone, endeavoured to arm herself with the fortitude necessary to support her with propriety and dignity, under the irksome visit, and painful suit of her authorized lover.

The

The trampling of hoofs, and the loud tone of the trumpets, echoing through the courts of the castle, seemed to declare the approach of the expected guests; and it was soon announced that Lord Viscount Broke, her father, attended by a few of his train, had preceded the Earl, who, with a long cavalcade of attendants, was then to be seen descending the hill, opposite to the eminence of the castle.

The Baroness, delighted and reassured by the intelligence of her father's arrival, preparatory to the introduction of the Earl, hastened to receive him, as he alighted from his horse at the great steps leading to the hall. Lord Broke, who tenderly loved his daughter, whom he had not seen for many months, embraced her with the warmest affection. But the overflowings of paternal tenderness were

soon

soon converted into sensations of the most poignant solicitude and lively regret, when the Baroness, throwing herself into his arms, entreated he would save her, if possible, from a destiny so full of misery, as that in which a marriage with Earl Ormond would inevitably involve her.

The good old Lord, who had pleased himself with the prospect of this projected alliance, which he considered as highly eligible, and to which he foresaw no obstacles, listened to this request with astonishment and distress. It is true, he had heard of his daughter's protest against a second marriage; but he had regarded it, as men are very apt to do, as the mere effects of grief upon a mind shaken by the first paroxysm of its sorrow, for the loss of a tenderly-beloved object; and, of course, had imagined that time would, ere

now,

now, have effected a change in a determination, which, as he conceived it to have
owed its origin to a sort of derangement
of intellect, would die away as the judgment might resume its functions. Nor,
indeed, could he easily persuade himself
that a Lady, beautiful and rich, and as
yet hardly three-and-twenty years old,
one too, who had once been the ornament and pride of the English Court,
could thus seriously resolve to hide herself from the eye of public admiration, or
with a constancy, inconsistent, as he
thought, with the character of woman,
that she would prefer the solitary state of
widowhood, shut up in an ancient gloomy
castle, situated among wilds and mountains, with no other companions than her
own vassals and domestics, to a gay and
brilliant court: he, therefore, smiling
with

with confidence in the truth of these his persuasions, mentioned that it must be impossible that she could enjoy more happiness in her present state than in the honours that now awaited her. He triumphantly expatiated upon the virtues and noble qualities of the approaching suitor, and bade her obey the commands of the King, and the injunctions of her father, and give him a favourable reception.

In vain, however, was every argument he could use; the Baroness could not listen, she could only weep in his arms, and with deep and suffocating sighs intercede for his pity, in saving her from the dreaded, hated marriage. "Oh, hear me, hear me!" exclaimed she, "my beloved father, when I solemnly declare, the moment that gives me to Lord Ormond will

will be the last of happiness and comfort I can ever know. And will you, oh! will *you*, my father, suffer your beloved daughter, your Gertrude, to be doomed to certain and irremediable misery, which it is in your power to prevent?"

" I should indeed be a wretch," said Lord Broke, " and utterly unworthy of being honoured by you as a father, were I to barter your peace to any considerations of worldly policy alone. But, look up, my sweet Gertrude, behold thy father. Do these eyes, moistened by womanish tears, beam aught but tenderness and affection? Oh, Gertrude, that I might but behold the accomplishment of the dearest wish of my heart—that I might but see my daughter's children! and not die mourning the extinction of a long line of nobles in myself."

" Oh!

" Oh, my father!" exclaimed the Baroness, " my dear, dear father!"

" Wait but the effects of time, my love," resumed his Lordship; " you may yet, impossible as it may seem to you, you may yet love a worthy and honourable husband."

" Oh, never, never!" cried the Baroness.

" Let me entreat you, however, my dear Gertrude," continued he, " to suspend your resolution, at least for the present; and let your own judgment decide as to this point. I have always considered your understanding as excellent; I know your feelings are delicately fine; but I think, with the fortitude you possess, you might so far surmount them, as to be enabled, in a short time, to think the man whom your sovereign has se-

lected

lected for you, may be the one you would
yourself have chosen. Nay, look not
thus piteously on me, Gertrude; your
father would persuade; he will forego his
authority; he will never command. I
will not say that Ormond possesses those
courtly graces, by which your sex are
often gained, and with which the young
and blooming Fitzwalter first lured you to
his arms; but let him not, on this account, be your aversion. Nursed on the
lap of war, and trained to feats of toil
and hardihood even from his cradle, he
has not had leisure, during the long con-
test between the Roses, to acquire those
graces and accomplishments, on which
many are inclined to place too high a
value. But, trust me, Gertrude, he possesses qualities far more noble, and of
sterling excellence. Amid the shocks of
                                        battles,

battles, he combats with undaunted heart ;
he has often fought, often conquered, and
served the cause he espoused ; and these
are actions of lustre to a Baron's name.
Such a one you may expect to find him ;
and, dignified, you may expect also, with
what in him I know exists in full power,
the purest principle of unsullied honour ;
and this, my daughter, far outweighs, in
sterling value, the flimsy qualities ôf
fawning gallantry, and smooth-tongued
compliment.   Should such a man be
pleased to take you, Gertrude, and who,
seeing you, can reject so fair a prize? the
Royal Henry (mark you, what clemency !)
gives back the forfeited lands of Fitzwalter, entire, to you and yours.   Should
you scorn his intimated wish, dread the
disseizure of your large domains, and
with poverty, perhaps a prison.   Such is

the

the prerogative of England's crown. *Dare not*, Gertrude, the danger; be not ungrateful for offered grace; nor think your father loves you not, when he urges the suit of the valiant Ormond. Rather doubt his affections, when he forbears to exercise the right of a father, and only prays for that compliance, which he has most assuredly a right to command."

Though language like this may seem harsh to the ear of a modern female, yet it seemed not so in ancient times of feudal authority. The Baroness, soothed, and even softened to a degree of sensibility almost painful, wept her thanks, and pressed to her lips the hand of him who had thus confirmed her liberty; when now the tucket sounded at the barrier of the outer moat of the castle, and announced the approach of the Earl.

Lord

Lord Broke instantly hastened to receive him at the steps of the great hall; and the Baroness, with aching heart, took her station at the oriel, and saw the troop of guests enter the court.

First, in procession, came six horsemen, with trumpets and bugles, two and two, followed, in like fashion, by six more, with pipes and instruments of soft music. Then came a knight, bearing the shield of Ormond, rich in quarterings, and emblazoned, followed by two ancients, bearing penons of silk and gold. Next, the Earl, on a grey charger, armed in mail, with thread of gold, his beaver up. Then followed two fair pages, one bearing his lance, the other his shield of battle. Then advanced fifty lances with their esquires, preceding and following twenty grooms, leading twenty sumpter horses

G 3 bearing

bearing the Earl's equipage. The whole
stood formed in lines when they arrived
at the great steps : first, the trumpets and
bugles, and next, the pipers, sounded a
salute; and then opening before the
Earl, he vaulted from his steed, and, followed by his two pages, and six attendants, he received the salute of Lord Broke
in form, and then entered the hall,
where the greater part of the castle
establishment stood, duly arranged by the
steward, in their best array. After a few
turns, and while a messenger was sent to
the Baroness, Lord Broke and a page
went to lead her in. And soon she came,
attended by her damsels and pages habited in her robes of ceremony, and
handed by her father, who, advancing to
the Earl, said, " Good my Lord, behold
my daughter, the Baroness Fitzwalter;
and

and my hope is, that, upon your mutual good-liking, ye shall soon be well acquainted."

The Earl, highly pleased with her modest beauty and grace, courteously bowed, and expressed his sense of the honour he then enjoyed; and the Baroness, in reply, gave, with tongue rather faltering, a suitable welcome to her renowned guest.

The nobles then retired, with their principal attendants, into an adjoining apartment, while the tables were covered, and then returned, and dined in the hall, at the chief table; while the knights and esquires of the Earl, and those of the Baroness, and the other principal part of her establishment, dined on tables below, on plenty of fish, venison, and fowl, and wine; while the minstrels, from the gal-

lery,

lery, regaled the ear with dulcet sounds,
no less than the eye was gratified with the
display of rich goblets, ewers, and platters
of solid gold, and the taste by the *gust*
of the most savoury viands.

The Baroness was relieved from the
greatest part of the trouble of the entertainment by the presence of her father,
who dictated the healths, though, sometimes, as he declared, at his daughter's
suggestion.

The Earl, who was seated at her left
hand, though lofty in his general demeanor, was greatly charmed with the
Baroness, and shewed her every possible
attention and courtesy. After a due stay
at the table, the Baroness and her attendants retired, and left the table to their
male visitors, who spent the remainder of
the evening in festive hilarity, in which
the

the health of their fair hostess was by no means forgotten.

When retired to her chamber, the Baroness had leisure to contemplate the character of her new lover. He appeared to be between forty and fifty; his figure, though majestic, was rather athletic than graceful; his countenance was open, and strongly expressive; his eyes were large and dark; his eye-brows thick, and finely arched; his complexion was brown, and its original colour somewhat deepened by a long series of military services. Yet, though with a person rather striking than handsome, and a total defection as to all those graces and accomplishments which distinguish the courtier, Lord Ormond, nevertheless, possessed qualities, which might have recommended him as a lover to almost any other woman than the Baroness.

There

There was, indeed, something in his appearance and manner not easy to describe, but which, to the eye of discernment, if not of taste, rendered him even more interesting than if he had really possessed the qualifications above mentioned. The Baroness soon felt easy in his society—she was even pleased with it; she, however, wished only to partake of it in the presence of her father, who, to her infinite distress, was obliged to leave her, to pursue, early on the following morning, his route toward Scotland, on the business of the embassy from the English court. The Earl was to remain at the castle till the return of Lord Broke.

CHAP.

CHAP. IX.

S'amor non é che dunque é quel ch'io ?

Ma s'egli é amor per dio che cora e quale ?

S'e buona ond' é l'effeto aspro mortale ?

S'e ria ond'è sì dolce ogni tormento ?

PETRARCH.

THE Baroness, amid the various incidents
and adventures of the two last days, had
not forgotten the mysterious minstrelsy
in the woods, and in the hope of again
hearing it, she waited near an hour in her
oriel. To her surprise, however, and extreme regret, the music, which had been
so constantly and regularly heard for

G 6   several

several successive nights, had ceased to
fill the wood with its sweet mysterious
melody: she listened, in the hope of
catching some faint sounds; imagining,
as it was now late, it might have retreated
to the more distant woods; but all was
silent; not even a note was to be caught.
Disappointed and perplexed, she retired
at length to her bed; but this incident
combined with other recent events to
prevent the approach of sleep; and having
wondered that it came, she now, with an
almost equal astonishment, wondered that
it came not.

A repose she so greatly needed at
length stole upon her senses; but owing
to the perturbed state of her mind, and
the various uneasy circumstances of the
day, it was short and disturbed; and she
awoke, with a terrifying apprehension that
she

she had been awakened by a noise resembling the clattering of some loose pieces of armour, the sound of which seemed to proceed from an adjoining room, the apartment in which the late Baron had formerly slept. This chamber, which was one of the largest in the suit which composed the western front of the castle, had, ever since the demise of the Baron, been almost wholly deserted. The Baroness herself had never entered it; and, except Winifred, who took care sometimes to open the windows, and, once or twice, to have a fire kindled, in order to keep the furniture from being despoiled by the damp air from the lake, which nearly environed the castle, no one had ever visited it.

The Baroness, for a moment or two, was so thoroughly persuaded of the reality
lity

lity of what she seemed to have heard, that she was no longer surprised that Sir Reginald should entertain the same degree of doubt and uncertainty relative to the appearance of the apparition he had described. For the instant, she was so entirely overcome with terror and apprehension, as to be rendered almost incapable of motion; the reflection, however, that almost immediately succeeded, of the apparent impossibility of her having really heard any sounds, soon restored her to confidence, and she again sunk into sleep.

The returning light of the morning served, in part, to dissipate the fears which night and silence had engendered; still, however, the Baroness could not persuade herself but that she had really been awakened by a noise, which she could

could only compare to the clashing of armour near her bed; and which she seemed distinctly to have heard, even while wide awake. Conceiving, however, it might have been suggested to her fancy by some dream, which she had ceased to recollect, she resolved to mention nothing of this circumstance to Winifred, or any of her domestics; and to endeavour to turn her thoughts from a subject, on which it seemed impossible for her to obtain either information or satisfaction, from any thing they could say, to one that more nearly interested her, the proposed marriage with Lord Ormond.

The assurances of her father, that he would not insist upon, or even allow her to be disposed of, contrary to her inclinations, if he had the power to prevent

it,

it, had greatly reassured and consoled her.
One task, one painful task, however,
awaited her, that of informing Lord
Ormond of her resolution of not entering
into a second marriage, and, of course,
her rejection of his offers, should she perceive, by his manner, he was likely to
make any.

The Baroness, although, independant of
a high degree of beauty, she possessed
more requisites for inspiring a strong and
ardent passion than, perhaps, ever before
fell to the lot of a single female, was,
nevertheless, so entirely free from vanity,
and all consciousness of superiority, either
mental or personal, that she believed it
possible, and even probable, that the Earl,
having seen her, might not greatly desire
the connection. It had been proposed to
him by the King, who had intended it as
                                    an

an act of favour towards herself, rather than the Earl; who, being directed to seek her alliance, by no particular motive of interest or ambition, but merely in compliance with the implied will of his sovereign, would probably, she thought, desire as much as herself, that it never should take place.

Whether she should immediately inform him of her resolution of remaining single, whatever might be the penalty of her disobedience, or wait till he should have made some disclosure, which might enable her to discover what were his real sentiments concerning her, remained for some time a subject for frequent deliberation. At length, she determined to preserve a silence, for the present, respecting her intentions, at least till she should have had another interview with the Earl, when,

when, probably, something might tran-
spire, which would afford her a further
insight into his real motives and designs.

Whilst the Baroness was indulging the
somewhat improbable suggestion that she
might herself prove as much an object of
indifference to the Earl as he was to her,
Ormond was revolving in his mind, whether it was possible so young and beautiful a woman as the Baroness might think
of him with the partiality he already felt
towards her; and whether a disparity of
years, and various other circumstances,
might not prevent her from experiencing
that strong affection, and tender interest,
which he conceived essential to the happiness he was come to court.

From the idea of forcing the inclinations of one so lovely, and, apparently, so
deserving, as was the Baroness, his soul
revolted

revolted with abhorrence and detestation. To have been voluntarily selected by her —to have been the object of her heart's choice, would have been bliss—would have been rapture! But could he hope? this was scarcely possible. " No, she cannot," exclaimed he, " *she cannot* love me! Yet, ashamed as I am, to acknowledge even to myself that I have thus hastily imbibed a passion, I thought, I hoped, at least to have resisted, till I was convinced it was mutual, my happiness, if not my peace, depends upon——upon what? a woman. Oh! shame, shame, Ormond! a woman thou hast scarcely more than once seen, and in whose averted look, and sorrowing eye, thou hast already read thy sad, sad destiny; she will not, *she cannot love thee.*"

If such were the sensations and reflections

tions of the Earl on a first and second interview, it will not be deemed extraordinary, on a repetition of them, observing the same symptoms of depression, and tender grief, joined to a behaviour even more distant and constrained, he should have resigned all hopes, if, indeed, he could be said to have entertained any, of making any favourable impression upon the heart of the Baroness, who, nevertheless, preserved in her manners the same courtesy and politeness with which she had at first received him.

The conviction that he must not hope for a return of the affection he had already conceived for her, was accompanied by a degree of sorrow and disappointment, which so short an acquaintance seemed scarcely to warrant. Impatience succeeded to regret; and he now re-

solved,

solved, by a declaration of his real sentiments concerning her, to put an end to a suspense that was already become painful; and now again overcome with a timidity he could not surmount, he determined to defer the execution of this design, till he could do it without that awkwardness and embarrassment, which he was sensible would attend an immediate disclosure.

The Baroness was not less anxious for a developement she at once wished and dreaded; yet, although both were equally solicitous for explanations, neither had courage to enter upon them; and Lord Broke had departed, and the Earl been three days at the castle, and several good opportunities had presented themselves, and yet he had never declared the purpose of his visit, or the reason of his stay.

Of

Of the former, she had been informed by her father; and with respect to the latter, her penetration had already made it most obvious, that Earl Ormond regarded her with feelings of no common tenderness, such as were likely to be the cause of much embarrassment, and put the strength of her resolution to the utmost test.

CHAP.

CHAP. X.

'Tis now the very witching time of night,
When churchyards yawn, and hell itself breathes out,
Contagion to this world.

SHAKESPEARE.

WHILE the Earl and Baroness were thus
the cause of mutual uneasiness to each
other, the rest of the inhabitants of the
castle were thrown into an universal terror
and consternation, by an alarm, spread,
as it appeared, by Ethelind, who, having
been dispatched by Winifred to fetch
some article of furniture out of the chamber of the late Baron, had declared she
had

had seen a figure completely armed, and with the visor down, standing by the side of the bed. Another of the servants, on passing along the gallery, in which the same apartment opened, had observed a light in the chamber, as of a taper moving slowly about the room; and had distinguished groans, which seemed to proceed from some person or persons in great agony of mind or body.

The terror diffused throughout the establishment, by the mention of these extraordinary appearances, however natural, was severely reprehended by Winifred, who treated it as a tale calculated to disturb the family, insisted that it was no doubt false, and declared that Ethelind should sit up alone, for some hours, on the ensuing night, in order, as she observed, to be convinced that the bugbear

she

she had raised was the creature of her own silly imagination, and to prevent the rest of the domestics from being infected with her foolish fears.

Ethelind, who still persisted she had seen something resembling, as she thought, in figure, the late Baron Fitz-walter, and who was really herself an object of compassion, whether what she had described was real or imaginary, from the terror she exhibited, could not really believe that Winifred, however violent and unfeeling, would execute her threat of confining her in this apartment. Her surprise and distress then may be rather imagined than described, when Winifred, at the hour when the rest of the family were retiring to rest, led, or rather dragged her, to the dreadful chamber—for so, to Ethelind, it appeared; where,

H

where, closing the door upon her, leaving her one solitary lamp, which served only to render "darkness visible," she bade her repose with the spirit of the Baron, whom she tauntingly assured her would not fail to visit her. Having pronounced these words, she drew the bolt of the large folding doors, and departed.

The poor girl, who had no resource, either in her prayers or entreaties, against the tyranny of Winifred, was obliged to submit herself to her fate, however hard. A flood of tears had somewhat relieved the overcharged heart of Ethelind, when, throwing herself upon her knees, her innocent hands clasped together, she addressed a prayer to Heaven for her preservation from the perils and terrors that seemed to await her in that awful chamber, which hardly even an angel from

Heaven

Heaven could have convinced Ethelind, after what she had either really seen or imagined, was not haunted and disturbed by the spirit of the Baron.

She arose from her posture, trembling, yet somewhat reassured by the hope her fervent prayers might be heard, and that no terrifying vision might arise to appal her.

Hitherto all was silent. Her lamp burnt dimly in its socket; and the beams of a waning moon threw a melancholy uncertain gleam athwart the gloom of the chamber. She arose; and partly opening the shutter of one of the high gothic windows, looked out upon the surrounding hills. As she gazed, the sky became suddenly overcast; the clouds flew wildly over the disk of the moon; the wind rose high; and the low muttering of distant

H 2   thunder,

thunder, accompanied by a few flashes of
vivid lightning, which, as it threw a mo-
mentary radiance throughout the apartment, seemed to give a horrible sort of
animation to the few objects contained in
it, conspired to overwhelm her with new
fears and apprehensions.

Oppressed by the extreme solitariness
of her situation, and the terrors that on
every side assailed her, the little fortitude
she had been struggling to acquire forsook her; and, throwing herself upon a
large old-fashioned settee, placed nearly
opposite the bed, she yielded to the ago-
nies that oppressed her heart.

While, with eyes still streaming with
tears, and a bosom throbbing with emotion, she sat, every moment expecting
some dreadful image to appear before her,
she heard a gentle noise, which resembled
the

the creaking of a door, turning slowly on
its rusty hinges, as if opening with great
caution. No door, or any apparent possible means of access into this melancholy
deserted apartment, except the large folding doors by which she had entered,
opening into the corridor, was, however,
to be seen.

Hardly had she time for conjecture,
when the loose arras, with which the
chamber was hung, became suddenly and
violently agitated; and the next instant,
while almost fainting with her fears, she
heard her own name distinctly pronounced.
" Do not be alarmed, Ethelind," said the
same voice, " it is only me." The voice,
she thought, was that of Edgar; but in
the next instant, the person who had
spoke emerged from behind the arras,
which was hung, according to the fashion

of

the times, at some distance from the walls, and she perceived, as she thought, the clown. "Oh! Mr. Motley," cried Ethelind, "is it you? it was very kind of you to come hither; for indeed I am sadly frightened."

"Do you not know me, my dear Ethelind?" returned the same voice, which she was now convinced was that of Edgar.

"Know you! yes," repeated Ethelind, with an air of surprise, which was immediately converted into the most animated delight; "but why do I see you in this disguise?"

"I procured it of Motley," replied Edgar, "who, after informing me of Dame Winifred's design of confining you in this apartment, a piece of cruelty I conceive to be almost unexampled, agreed to

to change coats with me; so that if Winifred should enter, which I conceive not
to be unlikely, if I cannot escape unob-
served, I shall be mistaken for the clown,
who, you know, may do any thing. I
visited this chamber some hours ago with
Motley, who was sorry to hear of Winifred's threat, and revealed to me the
secret of the concealed door by which I
entered; which, I believe, not even Winifred herself is acquainted with, as it has
been nailed up for some years, and is so
completely covered with the arras, as entirely to escape observation. We had
some difficulty in withdrawing the fastenings, particularly the large rusty bolts, of
which there are no less than four, but
finally succeeded in opening it, and for-
tunately without creating any alarm, the

Baroness

Baroness being below with the Earl, and the rest of the family too remote to hear the hammerings and knockings we were obliged to make, before our purpose could be accomplished."

"Oh, Heavens!" exclaimed Ethelind, "what if Dame Winifred should return and find you here! she said once she would keep me here all night, but I think she cannot surely intend to be so inhuman; yet if she should—if we should be caught —if she should really come back, and see you in this chamber with me——"

"Never mind if she does," said Edgar; "she will certainly not discover me under this disguise. Alas! what uneasiness has this ill-natured old woman already given us, my dear Ethelind!" continued he, "and how dear to me are these moments, these

these few short moments! for even hours
will appear but as moments, that I may
now spend with you."

" Oh! but the ghost," cried Ethelind,
" the ghost—the ghost!"

" I care not for all the ghosts in the
infernal world, ' exclaimed Edgar, with
energy; " what have *we* to fear? we are
innocent of any crime; and is not innocence a shield that will be always found
to be impenetrable?"

" Oh, Edgar!" resumed Ethelind,
shuddering at the recollection of her
former alarm, " had you seen this dreadful apparition!"

" I do not think you have seen any
thing, my dear Ethelind," rejoined Edgar; " believe me, it was merely the
creature of your own fancy, inspired by
the melancholy of your feelings, caused

H 5   by

by the cruel treatment you receive here, and the extreme loneliness of this castle, combined with the ignorance and superstition of those you sometimes converse with. Answer me, Ethelind, was you not first told by some of the inhabitants of this place, that the castle was haunted? such a report was, I know, in circulation, shortly after the demise of the Baron, and has since been revived, owing, no doubt, in part, to the unaccountable mysterious strains of music which have been lately heard in the woods."

" I have often heard that music, Edgar," said Ethelind, " but it was so sweet, that I loved to listen to it, and was never in the least frightened, no, not even if I were alone."

" But you have been told it was played by a spirit:"

" Yes;

" Yes; and I have often thought so too; for, if it was a human being, he would certainly, ere this, have been discovered ; beside, I think no minstrel but a celestial one, could play so divinely sweet."

" This, then, my dear Ethelind," said Edgar, " suggested the idea of a ghost, if not first to you, to some one, who has taken pains to impress you with the same opinion they themselves entertain. The spirit of the wood, by an easy transition, from the credulity of its inhabitants, becomes the ghost of the castle: this you have heard, and, it seems, believe."

" No, it was I—it was I that first said I had seen the ghost,' cried Ethelind; " and it was for this Dame Winifred resolved to punish me, by confining me in this chamber."

"And

" And what did you see ?" asked Edgar.

Ethelind described the apparition in the manner before mentioned.

" It is impossible," exclaimed Edgar; " it could not be !"

" Indeed, Edgar, it was really and indeed a ghost; I would not tell a story for the world; I am sure it was a *dreadful apparition.*"

" I cannot believe you really saw this figure, Ethelind, though I am sure you think you did. But why, in the name of all the saints at once, should it appear to you?"

" I do not know; but I am sure, Edgar, it did appear to me."

" It is impossible; the spirits of the dead, I am persuaded, are not allowed to revisit the earth; and if they were, why should they——"

He

He was interrupted by a loud groan, which seemed to issue from an opposite side of the chamber; it was repeated, and succeeded almost in an instant, by a noise which seemed like the falling of a coat of mail, or some large piece of armour.

Ethelind screamed, and seizing Edgar's arm, wildly exclaimed, " It is coming— it is coming. Oh! hide me. hide me——

" Hush, hush, my dear Ethelind," cried Edgar; " do not suffer yourself to be thus alarmed. All this may be nothing "

" Nothing!" exclaimed Ethelind, "nothing! Oh! Edgar, let us, I entreat you, let us leave this place. I shall die if I continue in it any longer. The door you entered will afford us a retreat through the passage to the western corridor; let us go this instant."

" By

" By no means," said Edgar; " such an escape would betray us, and subject you, perhaps, my Ethelind, to new insults and persecutions."

" But suppose the ghost should ap pear ?"

" It will not harm us if it does," replied Edgar; " but I do not yet give implicit credit to this strange relation of yours, Ethelind, though I am sure, as I said before, you most religiously believe it."

" Oh! do not say so, Edgar, do not say so, even if you do not believe it, or, perhaps, as a punishment for your incredulity, it will appear to us; and if I were to see it once again――Oh! Edgar, whatever may be the consequence, let us instantly depart. See how the lightning flashes along the chamber! It grows more and more awful! and, hark! what
dreadful

dreadful peals of thunder! Oh! save me
—save me from such a combination of
horrors as await me in this chamber!"

"If you continue to be thus agitated
and alarmed," rejoined Edgar, "you shall
go, let the event be what it will. But
strive, at least, to combat your fears;
believe me, when I say, they may not be
so reasonable as you imagine: a partial
gleam of light, serving only to throw the
remaining space of this chamber into
deeper gloom, and the accidental move-
ment of something shook by the wind,
rushing in from a fractured casement,
joined to the terror which had previously
taken possession of your mind, from the
circumstances of your having been obliged
to come hither unattended at a late hour
in the evening, might altogether have

3   conspired

conspired to suggest to your imagination the fearful spectre you have described."

" Well, but the groans, and that terrible crash we heard afterwards!"

" For these," pursued Edgar, " I can only account from the winds and storms of the night, in which we are apt to hear noises we cannot always account for. What we conceived to be a groan, might be a sound caused by pent-up wind struggling for admission.   In respect to the other noise, the place in which the armoury is disposed, is not, I think, very remote from this chamber; a thunderbolt, or even a powerful gust of wind, might have burst open some door, and thus, having free access, may have thrown down, with its violence, one of the helmets or coats of mail, of which

which I know there are several in the *casemates.*"

" But did not the sounds seem to proceed almost from this chamber?" said Ethelind.

" They did; so near indeed as to surprise me; as I believe the distance between this chamber and the armoury is a considerable space ; and the walls are of a stupendous thickness."

" It could not then be caused by the wind."

" I think it might, nevertheless. Although I believe what we have heard may hereafter be accounted for," resumed Edgar, " I own, I am yet greatly surprised, and confess should like to discover the mystery that seems to belong to this chamber, as also that of the music nightly heard in these woods. But I would now seize

seize a moment or two to speak of circumstances, in which I am more deeply interested, as more nearly concerning my future peace, to tell my Ethelind that her Edgar has no wish so fervent and so sincere, as that which he feels for her happiness, and that he would even die to ensure it.   But you are pale, Ethelind, you are still cruelly alarmed ; yet hear me, a few minutes only, and then, if you desire it, I will release you."

" I do, Edgar," cried Ethelind, " I do hear you," her cheek before, indeed, very pale, now flushed with crimson, and her eyes fixed upon the ground.

" I am very wretched," resumed Edgar, " and on your account ; I did hope, nay, I still hope, some time, your wished consent obtained, to call you, mine. But I am destined to be unfortunate. My father,
without.

without consulting my inclinations, is about to contract me to one of the most opulent of the Baroness's vassals; and I am threatened with his malediction, and even with disinheritance, if I refuse the marriage. To love the woman he has selected for me, is as impossible as it is that I can ever cease to love you, my Ethelind, on whom my whole hopes of future happiness depend. Our time may be short; I must therefore be explicit. I am resolved, whatever may be the penalty of my disobedience, not to consent to this alliance; I will still venture to hope my dreams of bliss may be accomplished: could I, my Ethelind, once hear you say you love me, half my griefs would be dispelled: to urge immediately such a declaration, might be wounding to your delicacy; let me then only entreat, if Edgar

is

is not deemed unworthy of its possession, you will reserve your hand for him, till he can claim it without injury to himself or you. Speak—speak, my sweet Ethelind, may I hope——"

"If I was convinced such an assurance would indeed give you pleasure," said Ethelind, again blushing violently; " yet if your father——"

"Oh, talk not of my father," rejoined Edgar, " he may relent; besides, I can now think of nothing but the happiness of calling you mine, even though the time should be far, very far distant. You will then, my Ethelind, preserve those valued affections for one, who, although he may first have to struggle with various difficulties and vexations, may hereafter claim you?"

Tears and blushes were Ethelind's only reply;

reply; they were sufficiently eloquent to be understood. Edgar took her hand, and pressed it tenderly to his heart. "And now, Ethelind," said he, "if you will, you shall depart."

"Yes; let us go," cried Ethelind; "yet, if it should be discovered that we have been here together——"

"Motley, perhaps, will befriend us," said Edgar. "But I have promised to release you, and if you cannot overcome your fears, Ethelind, I will."

While he spoke, they heard footsteps in the corridor. "It is Dame Winifred," cried Ethelind, "fly—fly——

Edgar retreated behind the arras; and before Winifred had withdrawn the bolts of the folding doors, which she seemed to do with caution, as if fearful of being overheard,

overheard, had departed through the door by which he had entered.

" Well," cried Winifred, who now appeared, " what have you seen to-night? has the ghost informed you of his reason for visiting this chamber ?" She pronounced these words in a tone of exultation, as if enjoying her triumph over the feelings of a poor, innocent, unprotected girl.

Ethelind, who was not insensible to this new insult, calmly replied, " she had seen nothing."

" Indeed ! ' cried Winifred, with a look of affected surprise, and, she thought, of incredulity ; " well, you may come out then ; I should not have released you so soon, if the night had not been so stormy ; you may go to bed then,

then, if you will, and inform the servants to-morrow that you are a poor silly fool, as you have proved yourself full of whims and vagaries; and that they must not, for the future, credit any thing you say."

Ethelind, who had no wish but to quit the chamber, hastily retired, without attempting a reply: Winifred remained behind, to close the doors. As she turned to take a survey of the apartment, she perceived a tall white figure moving slowly along, at some distance, without the arras. It turned—approached—glided by her—and disappeared.

Winifred shrieked aloud. At the same moment, a peal of thunder, which seemed to rend the heavens, burst over the castle, and seemed to shake it from its very foundations—the lightning flashed horribly through the chamber. The phantom

phantom crossed her again—and again vanished from her view. Another, and a louder shriek escaped her, and she sunk senseless on the ground.

On recovering, she found herself in the arms of Ethelind, and two other female domestics, whom her cries had drawn to her assistance. To the eager and busy enquiries of those who attended her, Winifred replied only with self-accusations the most astonishing, declaring herself to be the most presumptuous and wicked of human beings.

After many questions from her assistants, which Winifred was, for a long time, in no condition to answer, it appeared that she had seen the ghost, so generally believed to haunt the chamber of the deceased Baron. Dame Winifred, who had been the most incredulous, had seen it, it, and the reality of the appearance of this phantom was now ascertained beyond the possibility of a single doubt.

Amongst the general consternation occasioned by this incident, it will not be supposed that the Baroness could be long ignorant of so extraordinary a circumstance. She had left her bed in much terror and surprise, on hearing the shrieks of her woman, to enquire the cause of this disturbance; and having received all the information that could be given her, from those that attended her, had returned to it, with encreased astonishment and perplexity. More ample intelligence of this extraordinary incident was conveyed to her in the morning, by one of her attendant damsels, which was afterwards confirmed by Winifred, and various others of the domestics; for all who had any

pretensions

pretensions to appear in her presence, with earnest manner, and busy tongues, were eager in the relation of it; as also of whatever could possibly be supposed to bear any relation to the ghost; so that every circumstance of what had really happened, and a great many more, were quickly enumerated—the groans, the clattering of the armour, the appearance of the spirit, at one time armed cap-a-pie, at another wrapped in the dreadful livery of death, a winding-sheet.

To these superstitions, apparently so well authenticated, were added others, partaking of the ludicrous. Maclawney, the steward, who generally every evening enlivened his imagination with the necessary quantity of *hippocras*, which was a mixture of sack with honey, a draught in which Mrs. Winifred often pledged

pledged him, had seen the ghost in as many forms as Proteus himself could assume, or as double-seeing eyes, like his own, could possibly figure. It had appeared to Peter, the butler, in the shape of a butt of drink, in the cellar, and vanished in the twinkling of an eye; to Nicholas, the coachman, in those of a blue dog, and a white horse; by one, it had been detected in the person of an owl, vanishing in an ivy bush; by another, in that of a raven, croaking at midnight. These birds, ill omened as they are sometimes deemed, indeed haunted the castle; for a number of them having made their nests in the turrets, or among the neighbouring woods, they were often heard to scream, and flap their wings dismally against the windows. It was observed, from the instant almost

that

that the music ceased in the woods, the ghost began his nightly rounds in the castle: it was therefore presumed, and at length confidently asserted and proclaimed, that the ghost and the minstrel were the same.

CHAP.

CHAP. XI.

Oh, ye eternal Powers
That guide the world! why do you shock our reason
With acts like these, that lay our thoughts in dust?

LEE.

It was now utterly impossible to conceal
the circumstance of Ethelind's confinement in the chamber, or of her having
previously seen the armed figure, no
longer doubted to be the late Baron Fitzwalter, (though this had been Winifred's
declared intention) from the Baroness,
who severely reprimanded her woman for
her cruelty to the poor affrighted girl.

I 3

This

This Winifred endeavoured to excuse, on the plea of her having wholly discredited Ethelind's assertion, relative to this appearance, and of the seeming necessity of convincing her, and the rest of the domestics, of the absurdity of her wild fancies, for as such, she said, she had at first considered them; though she was now, she added, fully assured that something did really haunt that part of the castle, particularly the chamber formerly occupied by the Baron; although when seen by her, it had assumed an appearance quite different from that which Ethelind had described.

From this period, nothing but fright and confusion seemed to reign throughout the castle. Scarcely any of the servants dared go alone, even from one apartment to another, at any time, especially if they

in

in any way communicated with the
haunted chamber; but, at night, they
were quite paralyzed to any exertions;
and the business of the buttery, the dairy,
the stable, and the hall, were, in a manner,
neglected. The servants all found reason
to believe that the ghost had visited their
department. The pantler knew it by the
scattering of the bread, and the strange
noise he heard one morning, as he hastily
unlocked the door. " By our Lady,"
said the dairy-maid, " the ghost was last
night among the milk-pans, for all the
cream was gone this morning." The
grooms agreed, the ghost must have been
at night in the stable, and had been riding
the mare; for that when they went in in
the morning, the poor creature trembled,
and was all in a sweat; and as to the
hall, the ghost had made the penons

wave

wave without wind, the armour hanging up to rattle, and the stag horns to groan. Into one place, however, it was agreed the ghost had never yet been, the cellar: no one ever refused to visit that place. This forbearance of the spectre might be owing to the facility with which any one having occasion to visit that place, obtained volunteer attendants, owing, it may be presumed, to the privilege such adventurers had acquired, of swigging the tup, to put them into spirits against the spirit. Indeed, the plentiful use of good liquor now formed a very considerable ingredient in the regimen of every person in the castle. Mr. Maclawney took a double potion of hippocras; and Dame Winifred was frequently in want of a cordial, to keep her from the vapours. Hence it followed, that though the ghost did not

eat

eat or drink a morsel or a drop, in *propriâ persona*, yet it added very much to the consumption of the stores of the castle, and the expences of the family, and was of course a very expensive visitant to the Baroness.

The clown alone remained uninfected by the general contagion. He even sported with the fears and terrors of his companions; and had more than once been detected, in his attempts to encrease them, for his own wanton amusement, a conduct highly displeasing to the Baroness, who, reprehending him for his folly, insisted upon his desisting, for the future, from so unjustifiable a practice.

" Why, Motley," said she, " dost thou, for thine own sport, thus add to our present calamity, by augmenting the terrors of my people? and what is the reason that

I 5   thou

thou art inclined thus to mirth and festivity, at a time when others are racked with fear and amazement?"

"Again my reason! again requirest thou my reason?" quoth the fool; "in troth, a most notable demand! Prithee, Lady, give me a little of thy ugliness."

"My ugliness!"

"Yea, truly, thy ugliness."

"Thou talkest madly, fool."

"Not a whit: if thou, having no ugliness to give, wilt give me thy ugliness, then will I, being a fool, and *ergo*, without reason, give thee my reason."

"Thy attachment to thy fooleries," resumed the Baroness, "is even greater than the state of thy condition requires from thee. Thou art as much afraid of being thought any other than a fool, as the bulk of mankind are of being branded

with

with that title: and, in troth, thou canst not better prove thyself to be that which thou shewest, for dost thou not prefer folly to wisdom?"

"Yea, truly; as much as I prefer riches to poverty, drink to dryness, a good meal to an empty stomach, or a motley coat to a villanous ragged doublet; verily, I live by my wits, or rather by lacking my wits, which is the better of the two; for, having no wits to lose, I cannot lose my wits, and therefore cannot be frightened out of my wits by the sight of the ghost."

"Thou hast indeed the advantage in this," cried the Baroness; "and yet this is but the advantage of a stock or a stone."

"True, Lady, and, in so being, I am

the

the stoutest of thy household; yea,
verily, I am like thy castle, which, in
troth, I would thou wert; for, if thou
wert like thy castle, thou wouldst be
likely to keep thy castle, and not suffer
thyself to bolt from it, like a quarry
from a loophole in a turret, and let thyself be picked up and run away with by
any earl or knight of high degree whatever."

"Go to; thy buffoonery has been encouraged, till it borders upon boldness."

" Verily, Lady, these things are true,
and strong, and bold, and are therefore
bold in their outstanding, and less smooth
and courtly than might be wished. But,
nevertheless, since thou hast a most beautiful eye, a saintly smile, and a fair and
most sweet demeanor, mayst thou regard
them fairly, smile on them holily, and
receive

receive them courteously; and then the saddle would be rightly placed."

"Away, fool, thou growest muddy in thy fooleries, and art therefore almost run out to thy dregs. Beside, I am not disposed longer to bear with thee: go then, and be more discreet for the future; let me not again hear that my people have been disturbed by thy unseemly and most ill-timed jestings."

"Like the bride before the priest, I say, obey, and straight am away; and may both of us be fools enough not to fear stalking ghosts, and staring hob-goblins."

Not a day passed at the castle unmarked by some terrifying incident. Such of the Baroness's attendants as were obliged to pass through the corridor on their way to their Lady's apartment, which was in the

the same suit as that formerly appropri--
ated to the Baron, never returned without some fearful account of noises issuing
from the haunted chamber, such as loud
knockings, groans, and sometimes the
most dismal shrieks.

The situation of the Baroness, in the
midst of her terrified people, was indeed
pitiable. She could not, by any effort of
her mind, by any exertion of her own
reason, oppose or resist the universal torrent of terrors that now burst over her.
She had never been taught to doubt the
possibility of the supernatural appearances
of the ghosts; on the contrary, she had
imbibed tenets calculated to impress her
with the conviction that such were really
permitted, though she believed only in
cases of particular emergency. Nursed
and bred on the very bosom of superstition,

tion, within the walls of a convent, from
whence she had only recently been removed at her marriage with the Baron,
her mind had acquired somewhat of a
romantic cast, which the pageantry and
priestcraft of the religion of the age had
in no small degree tended to encrease.
The ardent affection too, verging upon
adoration, which she had conceived and
entertained for the Baron during his life,
and which, with all her natural enthusiasm, she still cherished for his memory,
had served to nourish in her mind these
opinions.

That the nocturnal minstrel, or, as he
had been usually called, the spirit of the
wood, was some heavenly visitant, sent to
watch over her, and sooth her griefs, with
the powers of celestial harmony, was a
sweet entrancing illusion; and when to
this

this was added the no less enchanting one, that this seeming wanderer of the woods was the spirit of her loved lord, her delight at hearing the music of his minstrelsy became altogether rapturous.

Widely different indeed was the state of her feelings at the appearance of the spectre, which seemed so alarming as to be marked only with horror. Had she listened only to Ethelind and Winifred's account of this extraordinary vision, she might still have denied implicit credit to the relation. But, when to these were added the recollection of the strange unaccountable noises she had herself heard on the night of the Earl's arrival at the castle, at which time the music had ceased in the woods, sounds which seemed to have issued from the very chamber in which the armed figure had been seen, as
described

described by Ethelind—when she thought too of Sir Reginald's dream, her apprehensions and distress knew no bounds.

The effect of these perturbations of mind produced an immediate change in her spirits, and she found it necessary to excuse herself by indisposition, from attending the Earl. This naturally led him to enquire into the cause, and, of course, the circumstances relative to the ghost were soon made known to him.

The Baroness, however, in her messages, made no mention of what had happened, nor did she afford him any immediate hopes of seeing her. She was, indeed, at present, wholly unfit to hold any conversations with her new lover, whose departure she now anxiously desired.

Her first resolve, on her dismission of the clown, whom she had found it neces-

sary

sary to correct for his levity and folly, was to send for Sir Osborne, her confessor, with whom she held a long conference in her oriel.

Having first given him a relation of every incident relative to this extraordinary appearance, with an account of Sir Reginald Harcland's dream, and every other circumstance connected with the subject of her present interest and deep concern, she requested his advice and assistance in her present distressing predicament.

The honest old father was overcome with a like astonishment and dread at this very extraordinary intelligence. "My daughter and Lady," said he, "this strange appearance, following the music of the minstrel of the woods, whom all our researches have not been able to discover,

cover, sheweth, most assuredly, the near approach of some mighty occurrence, relative to the fortune of the inhabiters of this castle; for the spirits of the departed are never permitted to pass the bounds of purgatory, unless for some weighty purpose; and when there is such a purpose, the holy saints plead for the indulgence of the solicitudes of the wretched spirit, anxious about the welfare of those it has left behind, and obtain permission for them to come forth, and signify their desires. But who is there, Lady, in this castle, of such importance as yourself? and who so likely to concern themselves about your fortunes as your deceased Lord? It must be he, and he only, who assumes these forms, to signify to you either his approbation or his displeasure; nor will his uneasy soul find rest till he has accomplished his design;

design; and what that is, Lady, you will eftsoon know."

The Baroness, terrified beyond measure to hear her own suggestions thus confirmed by her venerable confessor, the depth of whose understanding she erroneously conceived to be equal to his piety, paused for awhile to give vent to the agonizing feelings of her throbbing and oppressed heart.

At length interrupting his ghostly consolations—"Instruct me," said she, "most venerable and holy father, how to act; and, especially, how to deport myself toward the Earl, who, I fear, must be the cause of the distress of this perturbed spirit; is, perhaps, the object of the Baron's hatred; and whose visit and stay in this castle may afford the reason why his soul cannot taste repose.

" Though

" Though lost to me for ever in this world," continued she, " yet still the image of my Lord is ever present to my mind; the sacred resolve I then made, when the heart-rending tidings of his death first reached my maddening sense, remains, and ever shall remain, unaltered. Oh! hear me," added she, falling upon her knees, " if thou *canst* hear, spirit of the noble Fitzwalter—if thy perturbed soul is indeed sensible to the invocations of thy wretched widow, hear me when I swear, calling on every saint to witness this my vow, that not the acutest pang of misery humanity was ever fated to endure, nor death with all its horrors, shall ever compel me to unite myself with him, who directed hither by a sovereign's proud command, now sues for my alliance ; no,

3   were

were he even possessed of all the virtues
and manly graces that adorned thee, my
Fitzwalter, never will I become the wife of
this Ormond."

" *Swear !*" exclaimed a voice from an
unknown quarter, and in an authoritative
tone.   The father started up, aghast and
trembling.

" I swear !—I swear," pursued the Baroness, with a desperate kind of energy.
" Oh, Heavens !" added she, all her acquired fortitude suddenly forsaking her,
" it was his voice—it was Fitzwalter !
Help—help, holy father !" The monk, terrified beyond description, regarded her
not : but, after some pause, he called
aloud for assistance, though rather for
himself than the Baroness.

Winifred, who had heard the voice of
Father

Father Osborne, was the first who entered, and in time to save her fainting Lady from falling; other damsels of her chamber had also heard the call, and came, and helped to bear her to a couch, where she lay in deathlike insensibility; while they beheld the terrified confessor falling on his knees by her side, in an agony of speechless and bewildered devotion.

After some pause, Winifred hastened to employ the proper remedies, and the Baroness began to revive. But, with returning sense, the cause of her alarm returned also, and the words she first uttered were, "*I swear!*"

She was conveyed soon to bed, and, after a shower of tears, became somewhat composed; more so far than Father Osborne, who summoned all the rest of

the

the domestics to the immediate performance of mass, partly to quiet the
disturbed spirit, but more to be safer
from the alarming voice of the ghost,
amid the circle of society.

CHAP.

CHAP. XII.

Now, generous soldier, as you're truly noble,
Oh ! help me forth, lost in this labyrinth ;
Help me to loose this more than gordian knot,
And make me and yourself for ever happy.

LEE.

ALL this extraordinary bustle could not
take place without awakening the apprehensions of the family, and it was immediately whispered among every part of it,
that the Baroness and Father Osborne had
seen the ghost. So confident were they
of this, that each had determined in his
own mind, the form, the manner of its

K appearance,

appearance, and the business on which it had come.

The Earl, too, was, at length, informed that the Baroness had experienced some extraordinary alarm; but as to the particulars, he had not been able to obtain any satisfactory information. He did not fail to send anxious and respectful enquiries after her health; and, when he repeated the same in the morning, he was agreeably astonished, by a request for an interview with her in the anti-room of her apartment.

He had scarcely entered, when the Baroness appeared, supported by two of her women, weak, pale, and trembling, habited in a loose robe, indicative of every neglect of form and ceremony; while yet it displayed the elegance and beauty of her person, to which, however, she herself seemed

seemed utterly inattentive, being, to all appearance, wholly occupied by the sense of her own sorrows.

Hardly had he began to express the deep and tender interest he felt for her happiness, and his concern at her present distress, from whatever cause it might arise, when the Baroness was at his feet, conjuring him, in the most urgent and energetic terms, to forego all pretensions to her hand, for that now she was fully assured the spirit of the Baron could not repose in peace, while he continued her guest.

The Earl, although he had never entertained much hope of winning the affections of the Baroness, and had determined, with the most honourable delicacy, not to accept her hand, even though it held the wealth of kingdoms, unless voluntarily

K 2   given,

given, was equally astonished at the extravagant emotions evinced by the Baroness, and vexed at the strange cause to which he understood they were owing. But the agitation of his beautiful mistress, now at his feet, rendered reasoning and reflection impossible; and served to excite in his benevolent heart, a degree of tenderness and compassion, beyond what he had hitherto felt.

His first effort was a request to assist to raise her from her posture; but she, perceiving his purpose, when he caught her hand, exclaimed, with eagerness, " Never, never will I quit the humble attitude of a supplicant, till you, my Lord, all-generous as I know you are, free me from a condition so full of misery and terror! Oh, leave me—leave me; give peace to the perturbed spirit of my Fitzwalter;

and

and let me bless, even with my latest breath, the name of Ormond!"

"Little would you know of that Ormond," cried the Earl, with a tender, yet dignified air, "were you to believe he would suffer any interested or selfish motive to interfere with the peace of one, to whom his heart, even on a first approach, paid an involuntary homage. Rise, noble Lady, and hear, while I solemnly assure you of my ready acquiescence in any request you may form, though even at the expence of my own happiness and peace; but, let me entreat you to explain, what to me appears inexplicable, how my continuance here——"

"To you, my Lord, this circumstance must indeed appear singularly strange," interrupted the Baroness; "but know, this castle, once the abode of quiet and

K.3 uninterrupted

uninterrupted tranquillity, has, of late, become the scene of wonders, of alarms, of horrors, almost unparalleled ! But, first, my Lord, let me thank you, as far as language may enable me to express the feelings of my gratitude, for your generous, your noble compliance with my request; and let me also beg you to excuse an abrupt address, prompted, as I was, by terror and despair, to a violation of the established rules of courtesy and hospitality, and of that respect most undeniably due to your character and rank. Hear me also with kindness, oh, my Lord ! while with a heart gratefully confiding in your honour and goodness, I freely declare, that were it possible for me to have transferred my affections from my deceased Lord to any living object, and no insuperable objection existed why your suit should not

prevail,

prevail, I know no one, especially after the proofs you have afforded me, of an unsullied honour and the purest integrity, on whom my choice would have been more readily fixed than yourself."

"For this candid and endearing avowal, most revered and beloved Lady," cried the Earl, bowing till his knee touched the ground, " let me, in my turn, express my warmest acknowledgements. Oh !' added he, after some pause, and seizing the border of her robe, which he pressed respectfully to his lips, " had it been possible !—but no more, (laying his hand upon his breast with an affecting energy, indicative of a painful effort of self-command), it must not be—there is no alternative. Oh, Gertrude, Gertrude ! why— why so lovely ?" He stopped, rose respectfully, and recovering himself, after an-

other

other pause, courteously enquired the occasion of her sudden indisposition, and of the violent emotions by which he had just seen her so greatly distressed; adding, in a manner which rendered it impossible to doubt his sincerity, that she might command; and happy should he be, would the Baroness Fitzwalter accept the services of Ormond.

The Baroness, who felt herself much reassured, by the friendly offers and obliging deportment of the Earl, and was now become more composed and able to converse, gave him a brief detail of the mysterious minstrel of the woods; then of the armed phantom seen by her domestics; and, lastly, of the awful words uttered by some supernatural being, in the hearing of her confessor and herself.

When the Baroness had concluded her narration,

narration, the Earl, who had listened to it with much attention, and occasionally made enquiries respecting the particulars; thanked the Baroness for her condescension, in indulging his curiosity; and immediately observed, that most assuredly the whole of these events must be the tricks of imposture; and that some ill-designing person must have undertaken to excite alarm, for the accomplishment of wicked purposes. " When," said he, " and where is the ghost to be seen? let me be permitted to wait its approach, and, perhaps, I may be enabled to render you, Lady, some valuable service."

The benevolent Baroness, shocked to think that any person should experience any of those horrors she herself had so lately felt, shuddered at the offer, and painted the terrors of supernatural appearances,

ances, and the danger of those mental delusions, which they had the power to produce at will upon the strongest minds.

"Lady," said the Earl, "a soldier ought not to shrink from any danger, or cherish any fear. As such, I request permission to undertake the adventure. But recollecting that it is to free you from alarm, trouble, and danger, I must urge my request; nay, as a knight, I must not be denied, what I may surely claim as such—May I be permitted to see the haunted chamber?"

"Most assuredly," replied the Baroness. "My principal woman, and some others of my domestics, shall attend your Lordship in your visit, which may probably induce you to alter your intention."

"Never," said the Earl: and himself and his attendants proceeded immediately, each

each with very different feelings, to the haunted apartment.

The first care of the Earl, on his entering, was to examine the various doors opening into the passages, and other communications with the several parts of the castle; the bed underwent a scrutiny, as did also the arras, which, as we have before observed, was hung, according to the custom of those times, at some little distance from the wall. " All," says he, " seems orderly at present; the ghost is certainly not here now; but may perhaps be seen by one who may choose to honour him by attending his leisure, and that must be done to night."

" To-night!" repeated the Baroness, to whom the Earl immediately imparted his intention, " to-night!"

" Yes, to-night," replied the Earl;
" the

" the sooner the truth is known, the better; and as no man would wish to encounter too many dangers at once, I have to request that a fire may be kindled, that I may not be annoyed by the chilling damp of that room, which is by far the most formidable thing to be apprehended there."

The Baroness, finding he was bent upon his purpose, and that no arguments were likely to induce him to abandon it, proposed that he should be attended by one or two of his own people.

" By no means," said the Earl; " I would watch there alone."

" Alone, my Lord! Oh, think what may be the consequence !"

" I am fearless of all consequences," cried the Earl: " some mystery overhangs this castle, particularly that chamber, which

which I am resolved to investigate; and, from what I learn, the ghost has never appeared to two persons when together; and would not, in all probability, appear to me, if attended. Besides, if the ghost has really any serious business here, on which he comes, it is probably with me, and me only; as, from what I can learn, he did not commence his gambols previous to my arrival."

" My Lord," cried Father Osborne, who had entered while the Earl was conversing, " you ought not to speak thus lightly of things so solemn."

" Your courage, my Lord," resumed the Baroness, " is undoubted; but still, methinks you need not put it to such a test as this; as it can hardly be supposed that you are alone the object of

its

its visitings; but if it is seen by you, you know not how much you may be terrified."

"I will dare the utmost horrors of my ghostly opponent," pursued the Earl; "from whom, should he choose to render himself visible, I may hope to obtain some information highly useful."

"Good Heavens! my Lord, you do not surely intend to accost it?" cried the Baroness.

"Indeed I do," replied the Earl, calmly.

"Holy St. Agatha!" exclaimed Winifred, crossing herself: "but what if it should decoy your Lordship into some horrid place, and there leave you?"

"I will follow it, wherever it may lead," cried the Earl, "if, by so doing, I can but obtain possession of its purposes."

3   "Oh,

" Oh, my Lord !" said the Baroness, " let me, if possible, dissuade you from a scheme so rash."

" I will not only watch one night," continued the Earl, " but two, or even three, if I still think there is any probability of discovering what the ghost is, and what its intentions."

" My Lord," replied the Baroness, " I must cease my persuasion ; to oppose you farther, would imply a want of courtesy, unworthy your courage and your rank." The Earl bowed ; and again expressed his hopes that he might be able to render her the service he wished, by quieting her fears and those of her household ; and then, the Baroness being about to retire, respectfully quitted the room.

About the hour of midnight, the Earl, taking the key of the haunted chamber, repaired

repaired to his station. himself clad in armour, because he had heard the ghost came so accoutred, and bearing his trusty sword as his defence. The rest of the inhabitants of the castle retired at the same hour to their respective apartments; their minds all busily engaged by the subject of the Earl's enterprize, which seemed to them equally rash and extraordinary.

THE

NOCTURNAL MINSTREL.

CHAP. I.

—————Incedis per ignes
Suppositos cineri doloso.

HORACE.

THE Baroness slept little during the night that the Earl kept watch in the chamber, her thoughts being constantly engaged and harrassed by the subject of the day's adventure, which continued to excite in her the most uneasy fears and apprehensions. Every sound made her

B   tremble,

tremble, for every sound seemed supernatural ; she even feared to look around her, lest some terrifying phantom should appear ; and she more than once imagined she heard the voice of the spectre, repeating the word SWEAR, to remind her of the vow she had taken, and enforce her observance of it.   Morning at length dawned ; its cheerful beams served in part to dissipate her fears ; she arose while it was yet early, and having heard that the Earl had already left the chamber, she sent a message of enquiry by Winifred, which was answered by a request from the Earl for permission to see her.

This was readily granted ; and the Earl entering the room in which the Baroness was sitting, she eagerly but tremblingly demanded if he had seen or heard any thing,

thing, or had met with any alarm or adventure?

The Earl replied, that he had not seen the spectre, or any one of the figure described, which had rendered him somewhat doubtful of its appearance; but that he had heard·sounds, for which he was not yet fully able to account; and had therefore resolved to continue the watch till he should be able to discover whether the chamber was or not really haunted—a circumstance of which he declared himself very doubtful.

The Baroness finding the Earl had not hitherto been exposed to any extraordinary terrors or alarms, such as she had herself apprehended, made little or no objection to his proposal of revisiting the apartment on the ensuing night; and ac-

cordingly,

cordingly, at the same hour as before, he
repaired again to his station.

In the morning the Baroness renewed
her enquiries, and received from the Earl,
with whom she had another interview,
nearly the same answer as on the preceding
day. On her questioning him more particularly, she learned he had been surprised by the same noises which had been
before mentioned as having been heard by
some of the domestics, such as deep groans,
loud and frequent knockings against the
walls, intermingled at intervals with the
clashing and ringing of armour ; and
sometimes a noise as of something heavy
falling with great force to the ground.

These sounds were observed by the Earl
to have been louder, and much more frequent, than on the preceding night, a
circumstance

circumstance which led him, he said, to expect the appearance of the ghost, whose approach they seemed to portend, and whose presence he determined to await the next night in the chamber.

The Baroness, whose most terrifying apprehensions were again revived by the mention of these extraordinary and mysterious sounds, again remonstrated with the Earl upon his imprudence and temerity, in thus continuing to expose himself to the power of supernatural horrors, painted anew the dangers he might incur, and earnestly entreated him to abandon his design of pursuing the enterprize he had undertaken, on the following night.

The Earl, although he listened with a knightly courtesy to the Baroness's arguments, and was disposed to pay the utmost respect and deference to the opinions

of

of a woman he so greatly loved and ad-
mired, was nevertheless steady in his
resolution of penetrating, if possible, the
mystery that seemed to overhang that
chamber; and again, at the appointed
hour, though somewhat earlier than before, commenced his third night's watch.

The fire burned briskly as he entered,
and a lamp placed over the chimney diffused a cheerful light throughout the
chamber, exhibiting the figures upon the
arras, as well as of the carvings of the
old black wainscot, which covered one
part of the room. At some distance, by
the side of the bed, stood a large old
chair, covered, like the rest of the furniture, with dark blue cloth of gold. The
night was cold, for it had been stormy;
he drew it close to the fire, after having
secured by its bolt the large folding doors
by

by which he had entered, as also the window-shutters, and the doors of the closets, so that nothing could enter by natural means. Having secured, as he believed, every possible means of access, he took possession of his seat; and opening to an ancient legend, which chanced to lie in one of the closets, he endeavoured to amuse himself with the history of St. Dunstan, and several other persons of like religious eminence, in what he perhaps thought, but dared not call, sacred romance.

From these subjects he was, however, frequently drawn, by contemplations respecting the amiable and beautiful Baroness, for whom his affection was too tender, to allow him at present to experience perfect peace and tranquillity.

He

He had now been some time in the room,. and hitherto all had been silent, when a gentle knocking was heard at the door, which aroused him from a pleasing reverie.

"Who is there?" cried the Earl aloud.

"Bless your honour, it is only I," returned a voice; "my name is Peter; please you, my Lord, open the door; I have brought a little matter or two that may-be useful, and which Dame Winifred would have sent sooner, only being frightened, as one may say, out of her nine senses, for which she humbly begs your honour's pardon, she——"

"Come in, Peter," cried the Earl, who had now unbolted the door, "and let me see what thou hast brought."

"Yes, yes, you shall see," cried Peter, setting

setting down his basket, "your honour shall see. Oh Lord!—oh Lord! that you should ever think of sitting up all alone by yourself in this chamber."

"Truly, Peter," replied the Earl, "I am so much pleased with my accommodations, that I think it will not be the last night I shall spend in this apartment."

"Gramercy," quoth Peter, "not the last! why surely your honour does not mean to take up your quarters here? La! my Lord, only bethink you. Suppose now the ghost was to come from under the arras, or out of the walls, or through the key-hole, and stand in the middle of the room (erecting himself) as I do now, all over armour, your honour, from head to foot."

"I am accustomed to bear arms myself," replied the Earl, smiling, "and

should

should not therefore be more alarmed at the sight of a ghost in armour. But, Peter, thou hast not yet emptied thy basket—what hast thou got in it ?"

" In the first place, my Lord," cried Peter " a cup of hippocras, well mingled, of the best wine and honey, by Dame Winifred's own hands, such, your honour, as she keeps for her own private drinking; and Master Maclawney, the steward, swears none can be better, and he is a good judge. I have brought too some fresh logs to make up the fire, a lamp that will burn till morning, and a few cakes, all of which Dame Winifred, humbly begging your Lordship s pardon, sends to you."

" Well, Peter, thank Dame Winifred for her careful attention, and here is something for thy trouble (giving him a noble);

noble); this drink will help me to carry on a conversation with the ghost."

"This is a noble gift, your honour," cried Peter, who was a dry wit, "my dutiful thanks. And now methinks it is a great pity that so honourable a Lord should run hazard with this ghost; but saving your worship's honour, surely you do not mean to ask the ghost any questions?"

"Indeed, Peter, I do," replied the Earl, "and if it is as courteous as the ghosts of former days, I have no fear but it will answer them."

"Oh la!—oh la!" quoth Peter, "who knows, but if your honour was to speak to it, but you might fall down dead on the very spot, unless, indeed, your Lordship can talk Latin."

"Well, Peter, be that as it may," re-

joined

joined the Earl, " I heartily thank thee for the good cheer thou hast brought, though I probably should not have felt the want of it. I will not, however, fail to take it, as I had omitted my evening draught before I came."

Peter, thinking every moment of his stay subjecting him to the hazard of seeing the ghost, was by no means inclined to continue in the chamber, now he had finished his errand; he therefore, after laying a piece of wood upon the fire, and wishing his honour's reverence safe from the power of the devil, bowed and departed, running with all speed along the corridor, to seek safety in the company of his fellow-servants.

As the Earl closed the door, which was secured only by means of a slender bolt, the principal fastenings being on the out-

3   side,

side, the castle clock struck twelve. The Earl then drank to the health of the lovely Baroness, his cup of hippocras, and resuming his seat, again sought amusement by turning over the pages of the legend, which abounded with accounts of the conflicts St. Dunstan held with evil spirits, all of whom, however, he most mightily subdued.

" Well," said the Earl, " I wish I may have as good success with the ghost, who should, about this hour, they say, make his appearance."

The clock, however, sounded one, and nothing was heard ; and the Earl, wearied, as he conceived, by the tedious stories of the legend, and overcome by a drowsiness which he had long tried to resist, sunk into a deep sleep."

He was awakened by a loud noise, as of

of something falling in the chamber, and opening his eyes, beheld the very figure that had been described to him standing opposite to the chair, clad in complete armour, with its visor down, and holding in its hand a large truncheon, which it thrice waved, as if in signal for the Earl to arise..

Ormond, yet hardly awakened, was certainly much startled at this appearance, which, standing almost over him, had greatly the advantage in resisting an assault, and appeared, moreover, by the dim gleam of the almost expiring lamp and dying embers, a very formidable, because a most gigantic object.. Yet he viewed rather with surprise than horror this extraordinary nocturnal visitant. A moment made him thoroughly collected; and mindful of the purpose of his watch, he he started up, seized his sword, and boldly faced the strange phantom, who, seeming calmly to observe him, and, without betraying any symptoms of violence, made a motion for him to put by his sword.

"If thou art not mortal," exclaimed the Earl, "this weapon cannot harm thee; if thou art, speak, ere I strike, and ask mercy; declare thy name—thy purpose; speak, I command thee."

He paused in wonder and expectation. The figure spoke not, neither did it recede; the Earl raised his sword, and aimed a blow, but as he attempted to strike at it, the blade of the weapon, as if touched by some supernatural hand, shivered and flew to pieces; the hilt only remained entire.

"In the name of Heaven!" he exclaimed, while astonishment seemed to have

have almost palsied every sense, " who and what art thou?"

" Follow me," cried the apparition, " and thou shalt be made acquainted with the secrets and wonders of this castle."

The Earl, who felt a shuddering sensation creep through his veins, while the spectre pronounced these words, which were uttered in a deep and hollow tone, bowed and answered, " Yea."

" Hast thou courage, Sir Knight," resumed the apparition, " to accompany me wherever I shall lead thee?"

" My courage has never yet been questioned," replied the Earl, grasping with firmness his now shattered sword; " I am a true knight; I have offended no good power, and I fear no evil one."

" Thy sword is useless," said the spectre;

spectre; "but if thou art a true knight, thou wilt meet nothing in thy way to oppose thee. Take thy lamp only. and follow me.

As he spoke, the figure, gently beckoning, moved slowly toward the extreme part of the wainscot, next the arras, and not toward the door, which seemed wonderful to the Earl; nor could he conjecture how he could follow where there was no passage, nor yet, how the phantom could have entered, when all the doors had been fastened by himself.

The whole was indeed a mystery he was yet wholly unable to solve. He hesitated; but the promise of the spectre, and the hope of discovering the secret reasons of this extraordinary appearance, determined him, and he followed the wonderful invitation.

The

The spectre seeing him advance, approached one of the pannels of the wainscot, and touching it with the truncheon, it instantly opened, and shewed a long narrow passage. The ghost glided onward, still inviting the Earl to follow: almost petrified with astonishment, for a moment or two he stood irresolute.

"Fear not," said the ghost, "I will not harm thee. Thou art the appointed instrument of unfolding, by my means, the mysterious fate of this family, and this castle; be resolute, and proceed."

The Earl, reassured by these words, and urged on by his wish of accomplishing what he had undertaken, entered the aperture, which was wide enough to admit him without difficulty; and followed his ghostly conductor through a long suit of apartments. At length, they reached a

narrow

narrow stone staircase; the apparition still preceding him, and occasionally inviting him forward, the Earl descended the stairs. At the bottom of these, they crossed a small square area, when the Earl perceived on either side two large stone chambers, filled with various kinds of armour. They passed between them, and reached, at length, another flight of stairs, which they also descended. These seemed to wind for a considerable depth: when arrived at the bottom, the Earl earnestly demanded how far they had yet to go? The ghost made no answer, but with another motion of his hand, invited him forward.

The Earl halted, and taking a survey of his situation, concluded, from the extreme dampness of the walls, that they must have descended several feet beneath the

the foundations of the castle, and that they were now entering the vaults.

The ghost proceeded, without turning either to the right hand or the left, and the Earl continued to follow, till they reached a narrow passage, terminated by a portcullis, now drawn up, which led them through another passage still longer. In this were several loop-holes, through which the now dawning light gleamed faintly, while the air, with a full and keen current, threatened every instant to extinguish the lamp.

The distance at which they were now arrived from the inhabited part of the castle—the deep solitude of these vaults —the circumstance of his being alone with his supernatural guide, in the dead of night—the uncertainty whither they were going, and in what manner this sin-

gular

gular adventure might terminate, made the Earl, notwithstanding all his courage, secretly desire the conclusion of the enterprize, which was now attended, if not with danger, with horrors sufficient to appal the stoutest heart.

They had reached the end of the vaulted passage, and proceeded through a large stone arch down two or three steps to a spacious vault, which the Earl, on entering, immediately discovered to be the ancient burial-place of the family.

On a low bench of black marble were placed in order rows of stone coffins, an awful prospect at all times; but attended as the Earl now was by the phantom spirit, perhaps of one of the personages here interred, it exhibited a scene calculated to excite feelings of awe mingled with terror.

The

The Earl shuddered as he advanced; his blood seemed to curdle at every step. "'Tis horrible!" cried he mentally, and indeed a sight more appalling, or a situation more replete with horrors, than that in which he was now placed, can scarcely be imagined.

He stopped—he trembled; a chilling perspiration bedewed his limbs; for his mind had leisure to image to itself horrors still greater than those he saw; yet his resolution forbade him to shrink, or turn back, and determined him to go through with the adventure, even though it were, as he almost expected, to avenge the cause of some unhappy person unjustly, inhumanly murdered.

The apparition moved slowly along, and the Earl followed till they had reached the farther end of the vault. It then stopped;

stopped ; and. pointing to the ground, exclaimed, with a groan, " Have pity on an
unhappy injured"——This, then, thought
Ormond, is the grave of the poor murdered wretch, who lies buried in these
vaults. Lowering his lamp, he perceived
amongst a quantity of loose earth, which
seemed to have been lately dug up, a
large iron ring, fixed in a massive trap-
door of the same metal, partly sunk in
the earth.

The ghost made a sign for him to lift it
up. The Earl, setting down his lamp,
obeyed; and, after two or three efforts,
succeeded. Then taking up the lamp, he
observed several steps formed of loose
disjointed stones.

" If a valiant knight thou art," cried
the apparition, " and capable of pity for
the unfortunate, descend these steps ; and
thou

thou shalt soon meet that which will ease all thy present grievous sufferings, and yield thee a recompence suitable to thy deservings; for when thou returnest, thou wilt bear that which shall render thee superior to common mortals; and incapable of injury from open enemies or false friends. I would gladly attend thee, but fate forbids; my presence would mar the measure, and render my wishes vain."

" But hast thou not, mysterious spirit," cried the Earl, " other and more ample directions for me?"

" None are needed," answered the apparition. " But when come to the urn, scorn the gold, and take only the talismanic jewel. Be resolute—be valiant; and again, I say, no one in this cell shall harm thee."

The Earl, glad to find his adventure

was

was likely to have a speedy termination, and burning with curiosity to know what could be deposited in that place, instantly descended.

He had not proceeded more than twenty steps, when a sudden current of wind extinguished his lamp In a moment after, the trap-door was heard to fall, with a sound loudly echoed, as by some deep and spacious cavern. How to act he knew not; he proceeded, in hopes of finding the urn, but he was lost in the vast space into which the steps had brought him. He was bewildered; and stumbled over several masses of stone, which he found, on examination, were coffins like those above; and he consequently con- cluded that he was far removed from all human assistance.

He then, calling to recollection the

accounts

accounts he had had aforetime of magicians and enchantments, felt that he was now subjected to severe trials of his courage, and expected every moment to see some wondrous spirit start up, to tell his fate, and direct his progress to the mystic urn.

He sat down, and waited, and listened, but all was silence, except the occasional dropping of wet from the arch of the vault, to which he found himself almost continually exposed; and from this dropping he gathered that the vault was very spacious indeed.

He waited, and waited long, but nothing appeared; nothing was heard, except the dripping wet. He was wearied with expectation and inactivity; he wished he had not followed this phantom, yet he wished to see it rather than nothing.

thing.   To obtain another sight of it, he
invoked it to appear, by every mode of
address he conceived likely to have any
influence over such beings.   He called to
it, in soft, and low, and humble, and also
in loud, vehement, and angry terms;
but no answer was returned; all he heard
was the echo of his own voice sounded in
the cavern, and returning, and then
dying away in the dreadful distance.

" Alas !" said he, " this was then one
of those malicious spirits that are allowed
to torment the presumptuous; and I have
been presumptuous in awaiting this appearance, and in following its devilish
lures.   And I, for my punishment, must
sit a prisoner in this horrible dungeon.
But, let me not despair.   The door at the
entrance is closed; but, surely, I may
open it below, as well as I opened it

above.

above. Idle lamentations are useless and unmanly. I will seek the door, and Heaven guide my steps, and aid my efforts!"

He then felt his way cautiously by the wall or side of the place, and after clambering over many obstacles, thought himself happy when he found what he concluded must be the steps by which he had entered. They were so, and he soon found the door; but it was immoveable to all his efforts, however directed. He wearied himself with his exertions, but all in vain: at length, despairing of success, he seated himself upon the steps, thinking over all the hopeless miseries to which he was now exposed.

" And must I," said he, " die inglorious in this horrible den, lost to the world, and all means of serving my country and

my

my king? must my bones find no other
tomb than the iron harness in which I am
accoutred; and no other grave than
these steps, or the floor of the cavern
below? unhappy man that I am! and
death must be lingering and slow, and
come with all the sufferings of famine,
felt in these abodes of darkness. As yet,
however, I fear not death; but, shall I
always be thus bold? will not exhausted
nature bring upon my mind languor, and
horror, and fancied woe? Alas—alas! it
may—it will! Oh, wretched Ormond!
an Earl, noble and powerful, thou wert
within these few hours; and now thou
mayst envy the state of one of these insensible stones on which thou treadest.
Be merciful, Heaven! assist me, saints
and angels! But yet I will not yield till I
am quite fallen: while I have strength, I

will

will use at least my voice, to pray to
Heaven, and to call for deliverance. I
will explore this den too; and perhaps I
may find access to a place where I may
be heard : nor shall any thing but utter
inability terminate my efforts."

CHAP.

CHAP. II.

Then mass was sung, and prayers were said,
And solemn requiem for the dead;
And bells toll'd out their nightly peal
For the departed spirit's weal;
And ever in the office close,
The hymn of intercession rose.

SCOTT.

THE Baroness, anxious about the event of
the Earl's watch, had slept little during
the night, and arose at an early hour in
the morning, eager to make enquiries
concerning him. She was surprised to
find he had not yet quitted the chamber,
though it was then long past the break of
c 4　　　day.

day. After waiting some time in much impatience, she was informed that one of the Earl's attendants had been at the door, that it was still fastened, and it was supposed, his Lordship, after a tedious watch of several hours, had, at length, fallen asleep.

Another, and another hour passed on; and the Earl not coming out, or calling any of the family, her impatience began now to partake of apprehension, and she gave orders that he should be called; adding, that should he intimate any desire to repose longer on the bed, on which she imagined he might be reclined, she desired that he might not be disturbed.

The servant, dispatched with these orders from the Baroness, returned, after an absence which appeared to her extremely

tremely tedious, in the greatest distress and consternation, declaring that his Lord could not be awakened, and that he really believed he was dead. The Baroness, amazed and terrified by this intelligence, commanded that the door should be forced open, since so dreadful were her apprehensions respecting the fate of her guest, that no certainty, she said, could be more terrible than the suspense she now felt.

Her orders were instantly obeyed; but who can describe the universal astonishment, on finding the Earl was not in the apartment! and, as was still more wonderful and mysterious, from the fastening of the several doors, it was not to be discovered how he could have passed out; for the pannel in the wainscot, which had opened to the touch of the truncheon,

was

was closed, and every thing remained the same as on the preceding night.

The casements in the windows, which were of the sharp-pointed gothic style, were certainly too small to admit the body of the Earl; while the height of the chamber from the area below, precluded almost the possibility of his being able to pass through the windows, even had such an attempt been made, without being dreadfully bruised and mangled in the descent. The chimney too was examined. That indeed was wide enough, almost too wide for a passage; but no traces were discernible by which way; and, in fact, the chimney could only have led to the top of a lofty turret, from whence escape would have been impracticable.

The general belief, from these circum-stances, was, that the Earl had been borne away

away by some malignant spirit: and this opinion, together with all the corroborating particulars, were immediately conveyed to the Baroness. The unhappy lady was in a state little short of distraction at the information; and her distress was not by any means abated, when Winifred entered, wringing her hands, and exclaiming, "Woe worth the day! the ghost has run away with the Earl Oh! —oh! that ever I should live to be the bearer of such shocking tidings! what will—what will become of us! it will be said we have murdered him, and we shall all be executed without mercy!"

That the ghost could have borne away the Earl, however strange, seemed not to the Baroness to be utterly impossible; for she had both heard and read of such events; they indeed formed a part of the

c 6   creed

creed concerning ghosts, which was faithfully received in its fullest extent in the
family of the castle. Still, however, she
conceived it was more probable that the
Earl, bewildered by the terrors of the
ghost, had cast himself from the windows,
and was perhaps dead under the walls, or
had been tempted into the lake by the
fascinations of the spirit. She ordered
persons to search every where for him ;
and promised an ample reward to any
one who should bring her satisfactory
intelligence concerning him.

Meanwhile, she sent for Father Osborne,
who immediately attended, with a mind
fully occupied with terror at the intelligence concerning the Earl.

" He was, indeed," said the holy
friar, " too bold and presumptuous to
venture on the watch, without bearing
with

with him some holy relics, to defend him from evil spirits; but he did not ask for holy water to be used, as it ought, nor did he even sanctify himself with the sacred sprinkling, before he closed himself in the haunted apartment. So he is gone, by the power of the wicked devil (crossing himself) of a ghost—gone unshriven; and, of course, he now endures, and must long endure, the most cruel pains of purgatory; and the remembrance that all this is owing to his own wicked courage will disturb his soul, and it will come with clamorous howlings, and bewail its sin and folly, and thus add another ghost to haunt and disturb the miserable inhabitants of this castle."

" Oh, dreadful!" exclaimed the Baroness. " But is there no way of preventing

ing these horrors? I have heard of exorcising——"

"Great indeed," said the trembling friar, fearing lest the Baroness should require him to quiet these ghosts, "great is the power of the church over spirits: but the readiest way is to perform prayers, penances, religious processions, and masses, for the repose of the dead."

The Baroness, whose devout and enthusiastic turn of mind led her immediately to approve these sentiments and doctrines of her spiritual director, instantly resolved that these measures should be adopted; and that a solemn mass should be that evening performed in the chapel.

With the concurrence and approbation of Father Osborne, it was ordered, that all her own people, and those of the Earl, should

should attend the ceremony; and that the abbess of an adjacent convent, particularly patronized and enriched by many donations from the family of Fitzwalter, should be requested also to be present, and assist at the pious solemnities; and that the friar would himself bear the message, and obtain permission for the attendance of as many of the holy sisterhood as possible at the chapel   But before he went forth on his mission, she retired with him to confession, and spent the greater part of the remaining day in offering up prayers to the blessed Virgin and the holy saints, in behalf of the Earl; as also for the repose of the soul of her late husband, Baron Fitzwalter; but especially for the success of the intended religious ceremonies.

The monk, who, although with the
best

best intentions, had yet rather irritated
than composed the bewildered senses of
the Baroness, departed to make the necessary preparation for the approaching so-
lemnity, when the devotions of the Baroness were interrupted by a messenger
bearing a request from the youth Edgar,
for permission to take his station on the
following night in the apartment from
whence the Earl had disappeared.

The Baroness, filled with astonishment
and admiration at the courage and intrepidity of this young man, summoned
him into her presence, though with no
evident intention of assenting to his proposal, which seemed to her, after what
had happened, to be extremely rash and
madly daring. She replied to his request,
which he respectfully repeated in her presence, by representing the terrors and even
dangers

dangers to which he might be exposed by such an undertaking; and remonstrated against any further attempt being made to obtain a solution of the awful mystery, at least till she should have consulted with Father Osborne; declaring she would not on any account be persuaded to subject him, or any other person, to a situation, as it had proved, so hazardous; and if, on due consideration, she could ever be brought to listen to his request, she must first take such measures for his safety, which would exempt her, whatever might be the issue, from all grounds for that remorse she must otherwise experience, should the enterprize end as unhappily with him as it had done with the Earl of Ormond, whom, she added, should it not please Heaven to restore, she would for ever bewail with tears of regret and peni-

tential

tential sorrow, since she could not help considering herself as the unhappy, though innocent, cause of whatever misfortune might have befallen him.

Edgar, after various arguments, finding, at length, that the Baroness was not to be wrought upon by any entreaties he could urge to an immediate compliance with his request, which he assured her was of the utmost importance to the success of the undertaking, proposed that Motley and himself, with two or three of his Lordship's attendants, should examine the castle throughout; for that a diligent search would discover the Earl, whether alive or dead, if within the walls, where he might be detained by some accident; or by wandering in the dark, might have fallen into some of the subterraneous rooms of the towers: that this was the
more

more probable, since the search of many persons through the woods and dells of the domain had not been able to discover any trace of him.

Though it appeared highly improbable to the Baroness, if not wholly impossible, that the Earl could be concealed in any part of the castle, yet this request of Edgar seemed, upon the whole, too reasonable to be refused; and she gave orders that he should be permitted to search, attended in the manner he had proposed.

Every apartment in the castle, both above and below, every passage, vault, dungeon, and cell, every supposed possible place of concealment and confinement, and even the burial vaults, accordingly were searched, with the utmost diligence;

diligence; but no traces of the Earl could be found. The persons too who had been dispatched to make enquiries in the adjacent country, returned with no better success; and the Baroness, astonished and perplexed, abandoned every hope of making any discovery concerning the sad fate of her unfortunate guest; and turned her whole thoughts to the performance of those religious ceremonies which Father Osborne had proposed for the repose of the soul of a true knight, and loyal noble, who had miserably perished in her service.

Father Osborne returned about noon, with a benediction from the Abbess to the Baroness, and a promise of compliance with her request; and soon after sunset, the party from the abbey was seen wind-
ing

ing its way toward the castle, escorted by a party of archers and halberdiers, under the command of the seneschal.

They were received at the gate by the Baroness in deep mourning; and were conducted to a retired apartment to take refreshment. After the curfew, the bells of the chapel tolled mournfully for vespers, and the solemnities began.

Six monks of the order of St. Augustine, residing in the neighbourhood, as confessors, and employed in that holy duty by the Abbess, led the procession, each bearing a large waxen taper. Father Osborne followed next, holding aloft a large crucifix. Next came the Baroness, as a penitent, supported by four of her damsels clad in white, and four of her principal officers clad in black surtouts of penance. Then came eight lay sisters of the

the abbey, bearing on two biers the images of the holy Virgin and St. Bride; and next the choristers of the abbey, with instruments of music. Then the holy sisterhood, bearing, with downcast looks, a taper each, clad in black vests, and white hoods and scapularies, the habit of their order; and then the Abbess, mitred, and bearing a crucifix, supported by the chief officers of her monastery. Next came the attendants of Ormond, with downcast looks of grief: and lastly, the household of the castle in solemn train.

Thrice did they make the circuit of the court, the bell tolling, with chaunting at intervals, and then to the chapel, where each being placed in order, Father Osborne began a solemn requiem for the dead. In this the Baroness bore a considerable part, as chief penitent; she advanced

vanced reverently, and knelt at the steps of the altar, while the choir sung, the Abbess and holy sisters occasionally joining. As she knelt, the Baroness held in one hand a crucifix of silver, in the other her missal, and on her arm hung a rosary of beads. Her dress, like that of the nuns, was black. A long gauze veil, partially thrown over her, shaded, but did not conceal her face; for it was thrown aside to enable her to kiss the crucifix, and exhibited to the mournful beholders her beautiful eyes streaming in tears, while raised with a look of devotion, almost angelic, to a large image of the Virgin, which was placed in a shrine, with tapers in due order opposite.

The choir had now finished the first part of the chaunt: all was solemn silence; and Father Osborne approached,

supported

supported by two monks, to give her ab-
solution ; when, oh, horror! a knocking
was heard beneath, and deep hollow
cries seemed to shake the foundations of
the chapel. These in an instant engrossed
the attention of all present, and occasioned
a silence still more profound than the solemnities of devotion. The cries were
now, of course, heard more distinctly,
and seemed more terrible.

" Holy mother !" exclaimed the monk,
closing his book, and crossing himself.
The Baroness seemed scarcely to breathe ;
her female attendants screamed aloud.
" Our prayers," cried Father Osborne,
tremulously, " are not accepted : the
spirits of the dead are abroad : let us depart ; hereafter, by penances and prayers,
we may be prepared to meet again in this
place."

The

The nuns arose in disorder; the abbess raised her hands and eyes towards heaven, in silent and awful astonishment; the monk, horror-struck and appalled, hurried from the altar; and the Baroness, more terrified and more disconsolate than ever, was led back, almost fainting, to her own apartments.

Edgar alone remained behind, for he alone was unappalled by the alarming sounds; and he staid with the hope of being able to learn the meaning of the cries he heard.

CHAP.

CHAP. III.

His hoary beard in silver roll'd,

He seem'd some seventy winters old,

A palmer's amice wrapt him round:

*   *   *   *   *   *   *

His left hand held his book of might,

A silver cross was in his right.

SCOTT.

As soon as Winifred was again alone with the Baroness, after their return from the chapel, she earnestly conjured her, if she had any regard for her own welfare, for the happiness of her people, and desired that the spirit of the Baron should rest quietly in its grave, that she would immediately

diately invite Sir Reginald back to the castle.

"While that gallant and noble knight was here," cried Winifred, "this dreadful apparition never came to disturb us; nor were there any of those horrible shrieks and groans : nothing then was to be heard but the music of the wood, to which you, my Lady, so often listened, and which you used to say was played by some spirit ; and sometimes you thought it was the spirit of the Baron ; and then you would weep, and say how charming it was, and how much it consoled and delighted you."

"Ah! that music," cried the Baroness; "methinks, Winifred, it was certainly supernatural !"

"Who knows," continued Winifred, "if Sir Reginald was to return, but the

minstrel

minstrel might come again into the wood, and the ghost cease to haunt the castle; and that we might be as quiet and as happy as we used to be. You know, my Lady, the ghost told Sir Reginald he could not rest while the Earl remained here."

"There was something of this kind in the dream which Sir Reginald communicated to me," said the Baroness.

"The dream, Lady!"

"Yes, the dream."

"Oh, Lady, it was no dream! Sir Reginald told you so, because he was afraid, he said, you would be alarmed; but he assured me, over and over again, that it was not a dream; for he was as wide awake at the instant he saw the Baron, as he was at the time he told me of it; and that it was really his appa-

rition

rition that he saw; and further, that he
held converse with it, he thinks for near
half an hour "

" Ah!—so long! and what said it?"

" It said, my Lady, it should never be
happy, unless you would consent to
marry its dear friend, meaning Sir Reginald."

" Surely it never could say this!" cried
the Baroness. " Sir Reginald never imparted any thing of this nature to me."

" No, he says he did not tell you, my
Lady, all, nor half that the spirit said to
him; but he told me a great deal."

" Indeed! what did it tell him?"

" Why, how the spirit of the Baron
was grieved at your cruelty to him; and
how much he seemed to lament that you
should be so much prejudiced against

D 3   him,

him, who had always been so dear to him."

"It was then really a spirit that appeared to him!" cried the Baroness, shuddering: "did he declare so much? Oh! my Lord—my husband—my noble Fitzwalter, if without the sacrifice of that widowhood, now my heart's first wish, thou canst not know repose, let me but know thy will, and whatever shall be the consequence, I will obey. Oh that thy spirit, while it hovers near me, would come to me in my sleep, and instruct me how I ought to act, that thou wouldst advise, console, assist thy wretched—wretched Gertrude!"

She stopped: Her full heart was relieved by a shower of tears; and, while under the influence of the most lively sorrow,

sorrow, Winifred failed not to plead for her favourite Sir Reginald.

When the Baroness became a little more composed, she desired that Father Osborne might attend immediately, and Winifred instantly departed with this message; but remained so long absent, that the Baroness became surprised at her delay; and when, at length, she returned, " Why," said she, " is not Father Osborne come?"

" Goodness, my Lady!" cried Winifred, " I believe all the people in the castle are bewitched! here is a person arrived, who says he comes hither on the report of this ghost, a strange-looking old man, in a black gown, with a grey beard, and a large cap over his face, holding in his hand a long white wand, who declares he can lay this troublesome spirit; and craves leave to be admitted

D 4 _   into

into your Ladyship's presence; just as if, as I told them, my Lady would have any thing to do with wizards, or enchanters, and such wicked creatures: la, if I had not crossed myself when I saw him!"

"Where is this man?" cried the Baroness; "and how did he gain admittance into this castle?"

The porter, my Lady, admitted him, and Motley brought him into the hall; and there they are all talking to him, and questioning him, and, what is strangest, Father Osborne among the rest."

"Father Osborne! has Father Osborne then seen him?"

"Yes; and has been shut up with him, they say, for near an hour; for the stranger came almost as soon as we returned from the chapel; and Motley says your Ladyship must see him, and he is

coming

coming to tell you so; though I hope, my Lady, you will not, for who knows what he may prove to be? and as to his laying the spirit———"

" Well, Motley," said the Baroness to the clown, who entered, "what news hast thou brought?"

" Rare news—rare news, Lady!" cried the clown, jumping and skipping about, like a morrice-dancer on a May-day.

" Put less animation into thy heels, good Motley," cried the Baroness; "I am not disposed to be merry at thy fooleries, and let me know what thou hast to communicate."

" Yea, truly, lest my heels should run away with my wit, I will put on them the shackles of restraint, and gang solemnly like the ghost: yet, in that case would my heels be witty, though my head

should

should lack that which my heels had stolen from it."

"Thy heels will shew their wit in taking thee speedily hence," resumed the Baroness, "unless thou comest directly to the purport of what thou hast to relate. Who is this stranger whose arrival I know thou comest hither to announce? and what is his business in this castle?"

"To answer mathematically, that is, according to the square, *imprimis*, Lady, the stranger is a man."

"I knew this before: I ask thee only what kind of man is he?"

"Tall, and of a seemly and well-proportioned figure."

"No matter for his person; who is he, I say, and what is his business here?"

"Who he is, Lady, remains for *you to discover*; what he is, he is willing, with

your

your Ladyship's permission, *to discover himself*."

" What call you him ?"

" Truly, considering the nature of his profession, he may be said to have many titles."

" Ah! what are they ?"

" Some call him a magician, others an enchanter, others an astrologer, others a necromancer, alias a conjuror; and some, perchance, only that he is clothed in black, a white witch."

" Depend upon it, my Lady," cried Winifred, " he is an impostor. I never yet knew a man that had so many names, who was not an arrant knave at bottom; and we shall have good luck, unless you speedily send him packing, if he does not, by some juggling art of the devil, his master, hand off some of your Ladyship's

golden

golden ewers and platters; and then, by way of getting clear off the ground, help himself to one of your Ladyship's best palfreys."

"We will guard against that," cried the Baroness; "but what are his pretensions? what does he say he can do?"

"By his art, Lady," rejoined Motley, "he can do any thing, not otherwise within the compass of human ability."

"Can he exorcise—can he lay the ghost?"

"Yea, Lady, he hath promised."

"Witchcraft!—all witchcraft!" exclaimed Winifred. "Oh, my Lady, my Lady!"

"What says Father Osborne to this wonderful stranger?" asked the Baroness.

"That he hath knowledge super-human."

5   "Ah!

" Ah ! does Father Osborne say this?
What does he profess to know ?"

" Every thing."

" A sure proof, my Lady, he knows
nothing," said Winifred.

" Peace, wrangler," cried the clown,
" and let my Lady speak. I would thou
wert fast asleep on a feather-bed, and
might not awake to wag thy tongue again
these three days."

" By way of trial of his art, I would
first demand from him," resumed the Baroness, " some intelligence concerning
Earl Ormond."

" The Earl is safe, Lady."

" Safe !"

" Yea, Lady."

" Where? has he declared this ? if so,
Heaven grant he may be what he pre-
tends !"

" An

" An impudent and daring impostor, Lady!" vociferated Winifred, "an arrant and most cunning knave!"

" Hush, Winifred," cried the Baroness; " say, Motley, does he really declare the Earl is safe?"

" I have said, Lady."

" How does he say he obtained this knowledge?"

" By his skill in astrology, and the study of the occult sciences. He under-stands what every planet means to say, and hears the whisper of every constel-lation, knows all their houses, their ingress and their egress, and all the gresses; and can draw you the hieroglyphic of the year in the twinkling of an eye. All this he can do most featly; for he compre-hends all their motions and signs, and can call them all by their names; can mark you

you out the·star that points the toe of the
right foot of Orion, trace the milky way,
spy out Castor and Pollux, and shew you
Venus's girdle in the heavens!"

"Fool, Venus's girdle was never placed
there: but what said he of the Earl? be
quick, Motley, I am all impatience;
said he, indeed, he was safe?"

"Yea, truly, so he said."

"But where—where does he say he
is?"

"He will not satisfy you, Lady, on
this point, till he shall have had conference with you."

"Let him come hither then," said the
Baroness; "I would see this wonderful
stranger."

"Oh, my Lady! my dear Lady!"
cried Winifred, "he will certainly be-
witch us all."

"If

" If he is, as you say, an impostor, we shall have nothing to fear from him," said the Baroness.

" Ah, Lady! but what if he should prove to be something worse; if he should prove to have dealings where he should not have; and if he has not, how can he know more than other people?"

" Tell Father Osborne," cried the Baroness, " to come hither immediately; it is meet I should first hold some converse with that holy man; perchance he may not approve of my intention: in the meantime, Motley, go you to the stranger, and make some further enquiries about the Earl; tell him, if he will afford me some satisfactory information on the subject of this nobleman's sudden and extraordinary disappearance from my castle, I am willing, with Father Osborne's permission,

mission, to require further trials of his
art: depart, and bid the monk be here
quickly."

" With the velocity of an arrow shot
from Cupid's bow, and with more willing
speed than when it flew to pierce the
heart of the beautiful Psyche, I fly, most
excellent and sweet Lady, to infuse your
delectable commands into the ear of this
wise and most venerable doctor of the
arts of magic and divination, astrology
and conjuration; peradventure his beard
standeth not in my way, to intercept the
flowing eloquence of my speech, ere it
shall have reached the inner organ, the
ear being composed of certain labyrin-
thical windings and foldings——"

" Avaunt with thy tedious fooleries,"
cried the Baroness; " begone, and execute thy commission."

' 'Verily,

"Verily hast thou chid all my vivacity from my heels; and unless hocus pocus it come again—Oh! how these animal spirits flit about! now in the brain, now in the heels—verily are they now where they should be. Adieu, (jumping) adieu, sweet Lady."

"Whither so fast, Mr. Motley?" cried Peter aloud, addressing himself to the clown, who, having newly recovered his leaping faculty, was proceeding as fast as his heels could carry him, jumping and singing as he went along, from the Baroness's antichamber to the hall where he had left the stranger, surrounded by the assembled domestics, attended by Father Osborne. "Bate a little of thy speed, good Mr. Lightfoot, lest the ringing of thy bells should disturb the cogitations of the conjuror."

"Peace,

" Peace, fool," cried Motley, " and go thy way; I would my feet were half as nimble as thy jaws."

" Halt a little, though it were only upon one foot, good Mr. Motley, and tell us what says my Lady to this right wonderful man, this conjuror?"

" My Lady is a most wise lady; being wise, she accordeth to the dictates of wisdom; and in pursuance of these, she doth desire, command, and ordain, as it behoveth her high excellence, agreeable to her prerogative, that this stranger, being, as it is supposed, and as he doth himself declare, a magician, alias an enchanter, alias a necromancer, alias an astrologer, alias a wizard, alias a conjuror, this bearded sage, this gentleman of the black robe, this knight of the white wand, be summoned to appear——"

" *Before*

" *Before her.*"

" Who bade thee speak ?"

" Marry, I do not always wait for bidding. What then, does her Grace mean to try him by the ordeal of witchcraft, by having him thrown into the lake, to see whether he will sink or swim? Truly, I wish he may get well off with his conjurations, and none of us be the worse for them. But what say you, Mr. Motley ? do you think he can lay the ghost ?"

" I wish he would first lay thee, that stepping over thee, I might be rid of such a troublesome impediment: I am not sent hither to speak to thee, but thy betters. Go on, and tell Father Osborne to attend my Lady: my business is with the conjuror." Motley entered the hall.

" Well," cried the stranger, addressing him, " hast thou advertised thy Lady of my

my arrival, and the business that brought
me hither? and is she, moreover, willing
to admit me into her gracious presence?"

" Aye, aye,' cried several voices at
once, " what says my Lady?"

" Marry, that she is willing, with the
implied permission of the most holy
father, her confessor, with whom she is at
this time holding converse, to listen to
what thou hast to say to her; and further,
to allow thee to give her a specimen of thy
art, in quieting the disorders that reign in
her castle, through the turbulence of this
disorderly and most unmannerly ghost.
Nevertheless, supposing it to be the spirit
of her late husband, Baron Fitzwalter, she
desireth he may be dealt gently with.
Albeit, she first craves to know something
more concerning Earl Ormond, for whose
loss her Ladyship, though she loves him
not,

not, yet deeply mourneth, being in much dole and trouble of heart."

"The fate of the Earl," replied the stranger, "remaineth for the present suspended; let it suffice that he is safe; the spirit that haunts these walls must first be laid to rest."

"Well then, please your worship," cried Peter, "had not you better set about the job directly? I heard him, just now, clattering along the chamber, rattling his old armour about; and knocking and hammering against the walls, as if he meant to take a part of the old building along with him."

"I cannot proceed to the awful business which demands my attendance here," returned the stranger, "till I have seen your Lady."

"Suppose, Mr. Steward," cried Nicholas,

las, " while my Lady is deliberating, we were to hedge in a word or two for ourselves? what if I were to enquire of him about the steed? Sir—Sir——"

" What is your will?"

" Last night, an please your worship, one of my Lady's best horses was stolen out of the stable."

" A bay horse."

" Yea; the very colour."

" Having the near fore leg and the far hind leg white."

" The very marks."

" Standing fourteen hands and a half high."

" The height to an inch."

" Four years old, last grass."

" The very age to a day."

" Bought at Carlisle."

" Whey

" Whey (whistling), why, so it was, on my conscience."

" Now, pray, Mr. Conjuror, do you know what became of this horse? shall I hear of it again?"

" Thou wilt hear of it."

" When?"

" Now."

" Where is it?"

" In the stable. Thou wilt find it in the first stall, with a halter about its neck."

" Whurra—whurra!" cried Nicholas, " I'll go and see."

" I fancy, Mr. Conjuror," said the steward, " you have made free with the steed yourself; and so having returned it to the place from whence you stole it, are come hither to make a parade of your knowledge

knowledge, and to impose yourself upon us as a magician: I suspected you to be an impostor; and I now believe you to be a rogue."

" I know you to be a sot," replied the stranger, " and I suspect you to be a fool. Thou hast drank more sack and Rhenish within these three weeks, than would have served to drown thee."

" Say that again," said the steward furiously, " and I will pluck off thy beard, and knock thy wand about thy ears, till thou confessest thyself to be what thou art—an impostor, and an hypocrite."

" Peace, fellow, and be quiet."

" Do you not know who I am ?" cried the steward, striding up to the stranger, whom he eyed with a look of stern de-

E   fiance;

fiance; " do you not know that I have the honour to be the Baroness's steward?"

" Yes; and if I have any skill in divination, I know thou wilt not retain thy stewardship many days."

" Ah, ah, ah! (laughing) a good joke, a very good joke, upon my soul."

" Whurra—whurra!" cried Nicholas, who now entered; " surely, as I live, the horse is where he said it was, in the first stail; the very place; he knows every thing."

" In troth," cried Peter, " a most wonderful man! Please your worship, Mr. Conjuror, may I too ask a question?"

" What wouldst thou say?"

"There is a young man, your honour, the

the son of one of her Ladyship's vassals,
of the name of Edgar."

" What of him ?"

" This young man, an please you, Mr.
Conjuror, has fallen hugeously in love, as
one may say, with———"

" A woman."

" Wonderful ! how could he know
that ?"

" A young and beautiful maiden,
please your worship, who lives in this
castle, of the name of———"

" Ethelind."

" Her very name; a prodigious man !
Now, you must know, Mr. Conjuror, that
Edgar's father, being, as one may say,
well to live, for her Ladyship, God bless
her, oppresseth no one, he wont consent
to his son's marrying this girl, because,
forsooth, she is the daughter of a poor

cottager,

cottager, unless, indeed, my Lady should
command. Now, what I want to ask you,
Mr. Conjuror, is whether this marriage
will ever take place or no? for Edgar is
an honest young fellow, and beloved by
all who know him; and the maid is a
pretty girl, and as good as she is pretty."

" He will marry her in three days."

" Odsbodikins! so soon! egad then,
I'll go and tell Edgar, that he may be
getting ready for the wedding."

At this moment Father Osborne returned, bearing a message from the Baroness, desiring to see the stranger immediately: the latter accordingly arose;
and Father Osborne leading the way,
they repaired to the Baroness's antichamber

CHAP.

―――――――

CHAP. IV.

Yet so the sage had night to play his part,
That he should see her form in life and limb,
And mark if still she lov'd, and still she thought of him.

SCOTT.

THE Baroness eyed the stranger for a
moment or two, with a sensation of
mingled awe and astonishment. "I
have been told, venerable Sir," said she, at
length breaking silence, "that you have
the power, by some unknown art, to restore
peace and tranquillity to this castle, of late
most grievously disturbed and haunted
by a very troublesome phantom: if to do

E 3   this

this is within the compass of your ability, you will have performed for me and my household a mighty service; and, beside my most grateful thanks, you shall receive a rich reward."

" I shall on my part," said the stranger, " be highly honoured by your kindnesses. But before I enter upon the important business upon which I came, most noble and revered Lady," added he, " it is meet I first hold with you some private converse. With your leave, Lady, we must be alone."

" Alone! why alone?"

Father Osborne arose: " Fear not, Lady," said he, " I will return anon ;" and, together with the others present, withdrew.

" What is your will?" cried the Baroness, somewhat tremulously.

" Your

" Your castle, Lady," said the stranger,
" is said to be infested and much troubled
with a being of a supernatural character,
supposed to be the spirit of some one
departed."

" Truly, Sir, of late it hath been much
troubled."

" Have you yourself beheld this ghost?
and what form or appearance hath it assumed ?"

" It is said to have assumed various
forms; but most commonly takes that of
an armed knight, bearing, it is thought,
much resemblance to——"

" The Baron, your late Lord."

" It is so reported, as you seem to
have heard."

" Hath any thing occurred since the
death of the Baron, which may be supposed to have grieved his departed spirit,

and

and thus hindered its repose? Did you love him? Answer freely; you will speak to faithful ears."

"Oh, could I say how much!"

"And did you mourn for him, as widows should mourn, with deep, and earnest, and long-continued sorrow for his death?"

"Witness for me, Heaven, *what was my sorrow!*"

"Received you other lovers? this, per-chance, might grieve his sorrowing soul, and cause it thus to wander, seeking the rest it found not."

"None, by my faith."

"You have had suitors, Lady; did none of them succeed, and win your love?"

"No, none! my heart abhorred the very name of marriage."

"'Twas

" 'Twas strange, methinks; so young, so fair, so rich too, and so powerful! what, could no knight of honourable fame ere touch that gentle bosom, and awake in it love's genial fires?"

" Sir !"

" Pardon, sweet Lady, if I seem too bold. I have been answered. Your affections then remain unaltered; you have never swerved, even in thought, from that virtuous constancy in love, which proves it to be more than passion?"

" I never have; but why these interrogatories ?"

" Lady, they are necessary: these replied to, have you courage. to attend me whither I shall lead you ? Be not alarmed ; your safety is my care."

" Where wouldst thou lead me, stranger?"

" To

" To the chamber of your deceased husband."

" Ah! wherefore to that chamber?"

" 'Tis there, they say, at night the spirit walks; at midnight I begin my incantations; you, Lady, must be present."

" Me! Oh, Heaven defend me! the Earl was lost, who dared——"

" Courage, sweet Lady, 'twill be but for a few short minutes: the ghost must pass along, that's all."

" Ah! pass where?"

" Across the chamber."

" Oh, drive me not to distraction—to madness, stranger! Thinkest thou I can behold my beloved husband's spirit, and live? Oh, spare me—spare me such a scene of horror!"

" Thou

" Thou shalt not see it, Lady."

"How! not see it, though it appear, and yet be present!"

" No; for I ll tie around your brow a magic handkerchief, on which you must not look ere it be put on; you will hear, but see nothing."

" But why, I beseech you, tell me, Sir, must I be present at this awful scene?"

" If it is the spirit of your Lord that haunts these walls, it will not rest till it has seen thee; afterwards, it will repose in peace, and, its purgation ended, taste bliss immortal."

" If nothing but my presence in that chamber can restore peace to his disturbed and agitated spirit," cried the Baroness, after a pause of terrified rumination, " I will attend you."

" Thou hast spoken nobly, Lady,"

E 6 returned

returned the stranger; " and thy promise gives me hopes of success. Adieu then, for the present; I go to prepare for the awful moment. The reverend father may now approach. Fear not; the issue of these events may be most fortunate."

" Most fortunate!" repeated the Baroness.

" Be comforted, my daughter," said Father Osborne, who now entered, and observed the agitation of his Lady. " Assume courage, and confidently follow the directions of this learned man."

" What is the hour?" asked the Baroness. '

" It is within one of the appointed time."

" Oh, my heart!" exclaimed the Baroness. " May the holy saints and angels guard me!—He has said nothing more,"

6

at

at length added she, " concerning the Earl, at which I greatly marvel."

" The events of the night," said the father, " will probably unravel all the mysteries of the castle."

" Heaven.grant they may !" cried the Baroness; " and that we may be at peace ! But where is Winifred ?"

" Winifred," said the monk, " cannot appear."

" How ! cannot ! *cannot appear !*"

"You will know more hereafter," resumed the father; " her presence will not be necessary. Let me conduct you to a private oratory; and when thou hast repeated a few ave-marias before the shrine of St. Dunstan, I will fortify thee with the holy sprinkling; and then, when thou art thus prepared, Lady, I myself will attend thee to the chamber."

CHAP.

CHAP. V.

She heard the midnight bell with anxious start,
Which told the mystic hour approaching nigh.

SCOTT.

BEFORE these devout performances were well ended, the great bell in the tower of the keep sounded solemnly to the ears of the Baroness the hour of midnight; and leaning on the arm of Father Osborne, she moved with hasty yet trembling step along the cloisters, now scarcely lighted by the expiring lamp, and ascended the stairs leading to the haunted chamber. All was silence; yet she feared sounds that

that might alarm her at every step. Even the treading of her own light feet, and those of the unshod friar, seemed awful.

When come to the door of the chamber, they halted, and overheard the magician speaking his incantations. They waited a few moments, when suddenly the doors of the chamber unfolding, as of their own accord, discovered the magician sitting by the light of one solitary lamp, suspended from the ceiling; which, while it threw a partial gleam around, scarcely illuminating the farther parts of the chamber, served to impress the mind, awed by expectation as was that of the Baroness, with a darksome apprehension of mysteries already there. It served, however, well to display the dignified figure of the necromancer, and all the appendages of his art.

Before

Before him was a large table, covered with black cloth; and on it lay open a large folio volume, which he appeared to be examining with the most earnest attention. His right hand held his long white wand, his left slightly touched a dry human skull; by it stood an hour-glass; and before him a large animal of the lizard kind, and an owl stuffed and dried. On the floor around him were marked in chalk, a vast variety of mathematical figures, and mysterious diagrams.

The Baroness, since the death of the Baron, had never visited this chamber, without experiencing the most painful feelings. The thoughts of so soon being near an airy form, the only mode of being now remaining to him, oppressed her heart with a weight of woe, which dried up the source of tears, that season-
able

able relief to grief, and made her regard the solemn apparatus of the magician with almost insensibility ; although in other circumstances she must have beheld them with the deepest awe.

Her attitude was indicative of the most heartfelt distress ; her eyes were directed towards heaven, her hands clasped as in agony ; and thus she stood for some minutes, till a heavy groan, issuing from her very soul, seemed to relax rather than relieve her pangs ; and she sunk, almost fainting, against the shoulder of Father Osborne. A single tear now marked its course down her cheek ; and she, looking towards the venerable figure of the magician, faintly cried, " I am ready."

These workings of the most tender, yet steady affection for her departed Lord, had not been observed by the friar without

out the most friendly interest and compassion; and while he supported her with
one hand, he held out the other in an
attitude of exhortation; and gently exclaimed, with a tone of the most sincere
benevolence, "Yield not, my daughter,
to these mournful recollections; trust in
the power and mercy of the Supreme Dis-
poser of all human events; and may you
yourself experience that happiness you
come here to give to the soul of your
Lord!"

The magician, who had regarded her
with an attentive eye, from the instant of
her entering, now seemed with much
agitation to mutter some words to himself; then closing the mystic page before
him, he arose majestically from his seat,
and stepping forward, took up the ker-
chief, which had been covered by the
book,

book, and said, " The hour is arrived, noble Lady. All things augur well: close your eyes, and receive this magic bandage, which I alone can tie. Wearing this, none of the spirits that ever gave terror to the night can possibly appal or affright you."

" How long?" said the Baroness, tremulously.

" No questions, Lady," cried the magician; " we must be quick; the harbingers of my purpose I already hear. Kneel at this table."

The Baroness obeyed; and with hurrying hand, the magic bandage was bound around her head. " We are ready now," cried the magician: " support your charge," said he to Father Osborne, who took his stand close behind his Lady, ready to give her support if needed.

An

An awful silence succeeded. Low inarticulate sounds, like the murmuring of words indistinctly uttered, at length caught her ear. They ceased, and all was again silent. Suddenly she heard a noise like the bursting of a door, then of a rushing like the entrance of several people at once, and afterwards a sound, as of the clattering of armour. These too died away. She trembled; but was still. "Take courage, daughter," cried the friar; "the awful mysteries will soon be ended."

"The spirit has appeared," said the magician; "it has already passed along the chamber."

"Oh, my beloved, my adored Fitzwalter!" cried the Baroness, "when may death reunite us, by rendering me a spirit like thee?"

"Hush!"

"Hush!" said the magician; "the omens are favourable; attend to what is passing."

At that instant, the well-known strains of the mysterious minstrel caught the ear of the astonished—the wonder-struck Baroness. She started—shrieked!—tore the magic bandage from her brow, wildly exclaiming, "It is him—it is himself!" and sunk, panting, trembling, fainting, almost dying, with the wild emotions of her joy, into the arms of the stranger, (who had now thrown off his disguise) feebly ejaculating, as she fell, "It is, indeed, great Heaven! it is Fitzwalter!"

"Gertrude—Gertrude," cried the Baron, for it was the Baron, her husband, that now pressed her to his bursting, throbbing heart, "my life's best, dearest treasure!

treasure! look up—look at thy Fitzwalter. Ah! why so pale? Oh, save her—save her," exclaimed he, "fly—fly! unused of late to joy, this sudden tide, rushing thus unexpectedly upon her senses, is too—too much for feeble nature to support. Ah, why did I expose her to so severe a trial! But see, the colour steals into her lips, and visits those fair cheeks. Gertrude, my love, awake, behold thy husband, thy long, long lost Fitzwalter!"

" Methought I saw him," said the Baroness; " but tell me, (wildly seizing Father Osborne's arm) is not all this enchantment?" then snatching up the bandage, an embroidered handkerchief, " the same," said she, " I gave him at the tournament."

" Raise your eyes, my Gertrude," resumed

sumed the Baron, "and look around you; behold you aught now that resembles the ghost of your husband?"

"Heavens!" exclaimed the Baroness, "what is it that I see? a figure in complete armour! Ah! (recoiling) is not that the ghost?"

"Take off your helmet, Sir Knight," cried the Baron, "and shew yourself, in mortal guise, to this most virtuous and much injured Lady."

"Oh, spare me!" rejoined the Knight, "this hated, this humiliating disclosure."

"What do I hear!" cried the Baroness, "the voice of Sir Reginald Harcland!"

"The same, my dear Gertrude," replied the Baron. "The ghost I came hither to exorcise was the spirit of an unworthy knight, who, taking advantage

of

of a false report of my death, endeavoured to render himself the lord of yourself and your domain. When with faithful firmness you rejected his proposals, by the practice of the most dishonourable artifices, he attempted to terrify you into a marriage; and that he might be more free from the interruption of these his schemes, he prevented all communication on my part with you, by deceiving me with a false account of your death, the effect of grief, he said, for your loss of me."

"My Lord," cried Sir Reginald, "you see before you one of the most unhappy of men. I will not endeavour to conceal my faults; I will not even attempt to extenuate them. I loved the Baroness, and was directed to seek her alliance by no sordid wish of encrease either of pro-

perty

perty or power. The report of your having fallen in the ranks of the enemy, had gained universal credit and acceptance, before I even saw the Baroness. I alone knew that you was living; but hearing that the ship in which you had taken your passage to the Sicilian shore, was wrecked at the Straits of Messina, and that the whole crew had been lost, I was persuaded, nay, convinced, that I related a fact, when I asserted that you was dead

"The account I sent you before the report of your shipwreck reached England, that the Baroness was dead, had a similar relation to truth. She was indeed labouring under an illness, attended with the most alarming symptoms of danger. At the time I informed you of her death, it

F   was

was thought by some she could not survive many hours. Her attachment to her husband made me love her more. 'Ah! how faithful,' cried I, 'must she be to a living husband, who can thus love one whom she thinks dead! She is a prize I must not, will not lose. Fitzwalter is attainted, and never can return to be hers; it will be kindness to her to render her mine.' Thus arguing, under the influence of passion, I own, indeed, I became guilty of falshood, when I sent the trusty and well-feed messenger to say your Gertrude was no more. Ere she had perfectly recovered, I had the reasons above-mentioned to believe you were dead. I loved, offered myself, and was refused. You know the rest. This detestable scheme of the ghost was contrived and recommended

mended by Winifred, whom I had, from the commencement of my love for the Baroness, secured in my interest."

" But where," cried the Baroness, " is Earl Ormond?"

" He is safe, my dear Gertrude," said the Baron, " as I have already assured you. The noble Ormond, deceived, like yourself, by the treacherous arts of villany, has a few hours only ago been emancipated from a shocking confinement. Much yet remains to be explained.—With you, Sir Knight," continued the Baron, addressing himself to Sir Reginald, " it is necessary I should have some further conversation; till then, you remain a prisoner in this castle." He then desired that Edgar and the seneschal, who were awaiting his orders, would conduct him as a prisoner to a room in the round

tower

tower of the keep. " Lead him out," said he, " by the way he came."

The Baroness, whom joy and surprise had almost deprived of perception, observed now, for the first time, an opening in the wainscot, large enough to afford a passage for Sir Reginald and his guard. The dangers of those times when the castle was built, had induced the founder to contrive various passages and recesses in the walls of this apartment, either to afford the means of escape from personal danger, or to conceal whatever he held most valuable. But in the times succeeding, these recesses became useless, and were forgotten; and no one knew of the pannel so artfully constructed, as to fly open with a spring on the slightest touch, except Winifred, who had made Sir Reginald acquainted with the contrivance; and

and he availed himself of the secret, in the manner above described, to draw Earl Ormond from the apartment, who, conceiving the sudden opening of this pannel to be the effect of supernatural power, easily fell into the snare insidiously laid for him by the pretended ghost.

As soon as Sir Reginald had departed, the good old Father Osborne having congratulated the Baron and Baroness with tears of joy, they repaired to a saloon, where they were soon joined by Earl Ormond, whom the necessary refreshment, and a few hours sleep, had perfectly restored. The Earl's surprise, when informed that the Baron, who was universally supposed to have fallen in battle, was alive, and in the castle, disguised in the garb of a magician, may easily be conceived. The esteem and high admiration

F 3

he

he entertained for the Baroness, allowed
him not to mingle any selfish regrets
with the satisfaction he felt from the prospect of her again experiencing that happiness, of which she was so justly deserving, with the noble object of her tender-
est affection; nor did the manner in
which he expressed his feelings on this
occasion, fail to confirm the Baroness in
the high opinion she had conceived of
him.

The melancholy situation of the Earl,
on the departure of the impostor ghost,
has been already described. After having
made various ineffectual attempts to lift
up the iron door, through which he had
descended to this dreary dungeon of horrors, and having exerted himself in vain
to be heard, wearied with waiting, and
oppressed by hunger, he had almost relin-
quished

quished all hope, and had laid himself
down on one of the stone coffins, prepared to meet his seeming inevitable fate,
when he fell into a refreshing slumber,
from which he awoke greatly recruited,
and disposed again to use his reviving
powers, as also to pass the dreary hours
in again exploring the vault, his prison.

As he groped along the walls, he came
to a niche in which was an old lamp, and
behind it a crucifix, placed before a coffin
which stood on an end. He clambered
up into the niche to examine it, when in
reaching behind the coffin, it fell with a
thundering crash into the area of the
vault, and throwing down with it several
loose stones, crumbling with length of
time, he was beaten down; and had he
not been cased in armour, would have
instantly met the death he had expected.

I 4

He

He was, however, rather bruised than hurt; and instantly rising up, and retreating a few steps, he stood expecting that more of the wall of the niche might fall and crush him. Nothing of that kind however happened, and the echoes of the crash having ceased, and all being still again, he began cautiously to resume his examination of the niche. In groping over it, he found a piece of iron fastened into a stone, by which the coffin had been supported in its position; he found also that this stone was very large, and, as he rightly judged, must communicate with the other parts of the castle. He soon came to the steps which led to the entrance into this traverse; his progress in this direction was stopped by a massive door, firmly fastened, and against which he knocked, and beat in vain, for a long time.

time. He left it not without intention of returning, and tried his fortune in another search.

He now discovered by the side of the passage several niches, which were nothing more than small loop-holes now built up. Continuing his progress, he, at length, perceived, to his great joy, the morning light issuing through a grated window. Approaching it, with a full persuasion that he was now certain of escape, he found, to his great mortification, that it was only a window in a low apartment of one of the most advanced towers of the castle, and looked upon the morass forming on that part the boundary of the lake, so that it was not likely that any person would pass that way; and the strong iron bars, firmly fastened, prevented all hope of egress to himself.

Our

Our mortifications are generally pro‑portioned to the ardour of our expec‑tations. The disappointed and unfortu‑nate Ormond now found, to his extreme regret, that his escape was far from cer‑tain. The effect of the morning air was, however, reviving; and the light cheered his spirits. He looked from the window with pleasure, though that pleasure was allayed by the anxious wish for liberty, which he saw enjoyed by the birds of the lake, and the deer ranging on the opposite side of it.

Here he sat himself down, and conti‑nued his survey from the window, not without the hope of seeing some person who might observe his signals. But, at length, wearied with his dull watch, and overcome by fatigue, he fell into a pro‑found sleep, in which he long continued; and

and this circumstance prevented his earlier deliverance: for had not this wholly overcome him, he must have heard the call of Edgar and his companions, who undertook, as we have already noticed, to search diligently in every probable, and almost possible place, for the man, whose absence appeared to him most strange, and which the generality accounted supernatural.

That they did not search the range of traverses and subterraneans where the Earl was immured, was owing to the circumstance that these recesses were only to be approached by trap-doors, like that through which the Earl had been decoyed; and these, having been generally constructed with the utmost regard to concealment, were wholly unknown to Edgar, and the rest of the servants.

The Earl, after a sleep of some hours,

arose,

arose, still languid and unrefreshed; and retracing his way toward the lower dungeon, endeavoured to find some other door or chasm, by which he might ascend to the upper vaults. While he was busied in this search, he distinguished the sound of voices, raised together in chorus. It instantly occurred to him that the place he was in must be under the chapel; and that the Baroness and her people were at their devotions. The shouts and loud cries of the Earl, while endeavouring to make his situation known, were mistaken for the shrieks and yells of the spirit, that was wont to haunt the castle. and occasioned the alarm and dispersion we have before described.

Edgar, as may be remembered, alone remained in the chapel. To him the sounds he had heard seemed not to be supernatural;

supernatural; and he resolved to trace the mystery to the bottom.

Observing the situation of the chapel, he proceeded by a door behind the altar, toward the place from whence the sounds seemed to issue; and having reached the burial vault, he distinctly heard the voice of the Earl, calling loudly for assistance. Edgar having, with the aid of a shovel which lay in his way, cleared away a vast quantity of loose earth, which was thrown over it, opened the trap; and, in a moment, restored the delighted Earl to that liberty he had been long vainly struggling to regain.

The Earl, when thus escaped from the vaults, complained that the sense of the danger to which he had been exposed was become even more painful and oppressive than the danger itself; and as extraordinary

nary exertions are usually followed by proportionable depression, so the Earl now found himself too faint and languid to appear for the present; and he was earnestly desirous of being conducted to his room, where, having taken some very slight refreshment, he was left alone to his repose.

Edgar, delighted with having discovered and released the Earl, hastened to acquaint Motley with the news of his success, from whom he learned in return the still more extraordinary intelligence of the arrival of the Baron at the castle, and of his being disguised in it as a magician.

Motley, who trusted Edgar with these particulars, from a full persuasion of his integrity, and knowing that he might be useful to the final conclusion of the measures

measures now in progress, desired him, till the *denouement* of all the mysteries, to maintain a strict silence relative to these circumstances, as also of those concerning the situation of the Earl in the vaults of the castle; as it was necessary to the plans of the Baron that the Baroness, and the greater part of her attendants, should be unacquainted with these particulars.

After Sir Reginald had been led away in the manner above mentioned, the news of the arrival of the Baron flew instantly through the castle; and all the persons of the family, a few excepted, hastened with joy to behold again their long lost Lord; and to express, in proper terms, their respects on his return.

These forms were soon over; yet the Baroness,

Baroness, eager to learn the events which had led to her present happiness, thought them tedious delays to the communication of that important intelligence, which might convince her reason that what she saw and heard was not a dream.

CHAP.

CHAP. VI.

Breathes there the man with soul so dead,

Who never to himself hath said,

'This is my own, my native land!

Whose heart hath ne'er within him burn'd

As home his footsteps he hath turn'd,

From wand'ring on a foreign strand?

If such there breathe, go mark him well,

For him, no minstrel raptures swell.

SCOTT.

WHEN the Baroness was alone with the Baron, she gently reproached him for having so long concealed from her that he was still living. "Oh! why," said she, "did not you discover yourself to me

me on your first arrival here? why, disguised as a minstrel, artfully eluding my
strictest search, did you so often draw me
to my window, to weep and mourn anew
your loss, the memorials of which, every
note that vibrated from the strings of
your instrument, I know not how, nor
why, seemed to recall, and bring more
affectingly to my mind? Oh! why, when
it was in your power to have restored me
to the happiness I had, I believed, for
ever lost, did you suffer me thus to pine
in hopeless sorrow for your death?"

"You shall know, my love," cried the
Baron, "all my reasons for a conduct,
which, I am fully aware, must appear
extraordinary, perhaps not wholly justi-
fiable; for, oh! my Gertrude, how,
knowing thee, could I ever suspect thy
fidelity, how ever cease to rely, as I ought
                                        to

to have done, on thy angel-like, thy unexampled constancy! Oh, such, never,
sure before was there in woman,. most beloved—most amiable of human beings!" ;

" And did you indeed suspect my fidelity?" cried the Baroness ; " could you
be so unjust to yourself and me; as to
doubt it even for a moment?"

" I blush to say I did," resumed the
Baron : " like you, I was deceived with appearances; and not by appearances only,
but by representations, calculated to make
me wretched, even when my dearest happiness was in view. To explain this, it
will be necessary that I first give you
some account of myself since we last
parted. You now know my motive for
visiting Flanders. Deceived by the spe-
cious arts of an impostor, for such the
pretended Duke of York has confessed
himself,

himself, I took arms against my sovereign, and was obliged, by his success, to
fly my country, leaving thee behind; for
I could not wish thee to bear the miseries
of exile; and my title, estate, and honours,
were now at the mercy of a king, whom I
had offended.

"I shall not pause to relate the particulars of the various fortunes I experienced. I shall at present only say that I
entered into the service of Burgundy, and
fought in its wars. In one rencontre, I
fell wounded, and fainting with the loss
of blood, and was left for dead in the
field, amongst the slain. I was found by
one of those hardy adventurers, who are
wont to traverse the field of battle in
search of plunder; I won his attention,
and by him was conveyed to the house of
a Flemish mechanic who tended me with
great

great humanity and kindness. I concealed from him my quality and name;
and remained with him till I was recovered from my wound, which included a
period of near three months. In his
family was a young Sicilian, of a gay and
sociable disposition, who, to a remarkable
fine voice, united an extraordinary skill
in music.

" He often visited me, while lying soli-
tarily on the pallet afforded me by my
host; and amused me with the strains of
his lute, an instrument on which he
played so admirably, as to have acquired
great fame and reputation, even in
Italy. We insensibly became pleased
with each other's company, and he was
soon my almost constant attendant. As
soon as I was able to undertake the task,
I wrote to Sir Reginald Harcland, informing

ing him of my situation, and requesting intelligence from England.

" I sent this letter by a partizan, who ventured to return to England, in the disguise of a palmer.   Consequent on my connection with the Warbeck party, I dreaded, with great reason, the severity of the king, mingled, as it was, by his encreasing avarice ; on this account, to you, my Gertrude, I dared not to write; nay, I was restrained doing so, lest suspicion should attach to you, and bring you into danger. I received an answer to my letter from Sir Reginald, addressed to me by the name I had assumed, informing me, that as I had been returned in the lists of the slain, it was not doubted by any that I was dead.   He added also, that an act of attainder had passed the Royal Signet, which would subject me to certain

3   impeachment,

impeachment, should I dare to return to my native land; that Lord Stanley, the high treasurer, once the friend and supporter of the king, had been already arraigned, and was then under sentence of condemnation, his former services being quite forgotten. The same packet contained also the heart-rending account of your death; and the measure of my misfortunes seemed now to be full.

"I know not what passed for several weeks after this intelligence was conveyed to me. Death seemed now to have advanced nearer than when I lay wounded among the dead and dying on the field of battle. I wished not for life; I even prayed to be released, by a speedy dissolution, from a situation, on which the prospect of hope had apparently for ever closed. Time, though it failed to sooth

my

my griefs, yet gave me back to health. I
determined to quit Flanders; and careless
whither I went, proposed to accompany
my Sicilian friend, in his purposed expedition to Palermo.

" He received my proposal of accompanying him with unfeigned expressions
of joy; and we crossed through France,
and embarking at Marseilles, sailed for the
coast of Sicily. I wrote to Sir Reginald,
previous to my embarkation, acquainting
him with the place of my destination, as
also my resolution of never more visiting
England.

" Our vessel was wrecked at the Straits
of Messina, and most of the ship's crew
perished with it. My friend the Sicilian,
myself, with two others, alone escaped;
but we both lost nearly our all. My
companion now proved indeed my friend,

for

for by his skill in music he earned enough
to prevent me, as well as himself, from
starving. His employment as a minstrel
was indeed tolerably profitable; and it
became more so, when he had taught me
to accompany him in his performances.

" By continued practice, I became a
good proficient in the art; and those me-
lodies which occasioned such delight and
surprise in you, for a. considerable time
won my bread. Yet though thus employed my attention, and I was much
amused with the scenes and manners of
the finest country, and most polished
people in the world, yet neither time nor
amusement could extinguish the grief I
felt for the loss of my beloved Gertrude;
and the hours passed often mournfully,
and heavily along. I accused my folly as
the cause of your death; and a thousand

times

times execrated that fatal credulity, which had drawn me from my paternal abode—from all that was precious to me on earth, had involved me in irremediable ruin, and perpetual banishment from my native soil. 'Oh, England!' I exclaimed, ' my beloved country! the scene of my former joys, the abode of my honourable ancestors, how hard my fortune, which bids me not dare to behold you more!'

" Such often were my melancholy reflections, and sad regrets ; when, at length, one day falling accidentally into company with some English traders, who had come to the marts of Italy, to purchase the rich commodities of India, either from Aleppo in Syria, or Alexandria in Egypt, I learnt that a general pardon had been afforded to all such of the English nobility as had been attainted

for

for taking up arms in the cause of Warbeck, provided they returned within a
limited time, and took the oaths of allegiance to King Henry.

'What pity,' said one of them, who
was a North countryman, 'that Lord Fitzwalter, one of the noblest of our Northern
Barons, should have fallen into the snares
of that impostor! Had he lived, they say,
the king would have pardoned him, as
well for the sake of the lovely Baroness of
the family of Broke, of which this fair
widow is sole heiress, as also from a
persuasion that he was not actuated
by that factious spirit which induced
many of the partizans of Warbeck to take
up arms.'

" Hearing this, I observed, with affected
indifference—'It is well your king is mer-

ciful;

ciful; and that peace is restored to England, which has long suffered all the evils of civil war. But why should the king be inclined to spare Lord Fitzwalter on account of his wife, who, I heard at the Court of Burgundy, had not survived the death of the Baron?'

'In that,' said my countryman, 'you have been misinformed. She did grieve, indeed, as women always will, when disappointed in their comforts by the loss of a good husband: but young widows, with good estates, need not mourn long: and I dare say the Baroness cares not a fig for the Baron now; for she is about to make up her loss, by giving her willing hand, and rich Barony of Fitzwalter, which, by a grant from the king, she is allowed to hold during her life, to a gay, gallant

lant young knight, Sir Reginald Harcland, a kinsman of her late Lord's.'

" I started at this intelligence, though
it was yet impossible to give credit to it.
' Have you,' said I, ' so recently left England, and know not that the Baroness Fitzwalter has been dead some months?'

' Indeed !' replied my countryman,
sarcastically, 'she dead! where, pray, did
you gather that information? but let me
observe, by whatever channel you obtained
it, it is false.'—' Aye, truly,' cried another
of the merchants, 'for, to my knowledge,
the Baroness was alive and well, some
weeks since; and the Knight, Sir Reginald, was at her castle, laying close siege
to the buxom widow, I do assure you.
But some people are of opinion that the
king will not allow her to marry him, and
that he intends to send her a husband

from

from court; and he, or any one else, I
dare say, will be equally acceptable.'

" It is in vain to describe my emotions,
at the moment I received this intelligence
and these remarks; you, then, my Gertrude, was living, strange and unaccountable as it appeared; but I was yet in
danger of losing you for ever; and, what
I felt still more cruelly, you had forgot
Fitzwalter, and waited, with indelicate
willingness, the proposals of another
suitor. My attainder had been revoked,
in common with the rest of my partizans.
Nothing now opposed my return. A conviction of the perfidy of the man, by
whom I had been thus cruelly deceived,
flashed at once upon my mind. I staid
not to hear more—I flew out of the room,
and taking a hurried adieu of my Sicilian
acquaintance, to whom I now discovered
                                    myself,

myself I won my way homeward in the character of a minstrel, and embarked at Calais for England.

" My heart rejoiced when I set my foot upon English ground; and though disguised and unknown, I seemed to be among friends. But what, oh Gertrude! were my emotions, on beholding the towers of my castle, and those walls in which you resided! I could scarce refrain from hastening to your presence, and claiming your love; but the conversation of the merchants in Italy had excited in me painful doubts and racking fears respecting you; and these were not done away, by the enquiries I made as I approached my home. I resolved, before I made myself known, to discover the true state of your affections and character, and of the conduct of Sir Reginald, of

whose

whose treachery, however, I could entertain no doubt.

" With this view, I entered the wood; and with the sound of my lute, endeavoured to draw some one of your people, whom curiosity might direct, to the place of my retreat; and to such one, if faithful, I resolved to make myself known.

" I repaired, for three or four nights together, to the wood, without seeing any but strangers, whom I cautiously avoided; concealing myself, on their approach, behind the boles of the trees, or beneath the underwood, or among the rocks. My impatience could ill brook the delay, and I began to be weary of my nocturnal ramblings; and was inclined to have abandoned my purpose, and make my way to the castle, and either upbraid or adore you, as I might see occasion.

" Accident,

" Accident, however, or the curiosity I had excited, at last befriended me : Motley came into the wood. I, knowing the integrity of his character, discovered myself. His surprise at first partook of terror; for he, like all others, believed that I was dead. He could scarcely persuade himself that I was a living being : but these doubts and apprehensions were soon converted into sensations of the sincerest joy, when he was convinced that I was really his former master. From him I gained all the intelligence I could desire, and particularly he afforded me the most heartfelt delight, on assuring me that you, my Gertrude, really mourned, even then, for my loss.

" As, however, I had proceeded thus far in my scheme, and thinking, excuse me, most adored of women, that he might

possibly

possibly be mistaken, desirous also of knowing how you would act toward the Earl of Ormond, I determined to wait the result; and therefore I continued my minstrelsy, which served as a signal to Motley, and afterwards to two or three faithful domestics, to visit me, and communicate intelligence. Motley was directed to trust my secret with several; for by that means the communication with me might be carried on more securely.

" By Motley I was informed of the departure, or rather dismissal, of Sir Reginald, and the arrival also of Lord Ormond; and that you conducted yourself to him exactly as I could have desired. I learned also from him, of the still more extraordinary circumstance of the ghost, which immediately, on the supposed departure

parture of Sir Reginald, began his nightly disturbances.

" I had some reason to suspect that the ghost was no other than Sir Reginald; and in this opinion I was soon confirmed, by the observations made at my direction by my friend Motley, who, although by profession a fool, I now found to be by far the most reasonable person in the family.

" He told me that Winifred had been observed to go often toward what was called the haunted apartment; and I desired him to watch her closely. He did so; and found that the ghost entered the chamber by a secret door formed in the wainscot: he found also, what they did not know, that another door opened behind the arras, which hanging, in the usual manner, at a distance from the wall,

enabled

enabled him to overhear a conversation between Winifred and the pretended ghost, who was really Sir Reginald, in which the base-measures he took to secure your hand were made most evident. One night, Motley covered himself with a white sheet, and issuing from his conceal-ment behind the arras, at the same mo-ment that a loud peal of thunder rolled over the towers of the castle, Winifred, persuaded that she had now really seen a ghost, come, as she imagined, to punish her for her presumption, shrieked and fell into fits.

" This adventure might have been pro-ductive of some salutary effect upon the mind of Winifred, had not a disclosure of the real circumstance been made to her by Sir Reginald, who had the means of seeing and hearing all that passed.

3   " By

" By Motley I was also informed of the harsh conduct of Winifred toward poor Ethelind, which proves her cruel as well as base. The sudden disappearance of the Earl of Ormond, for which I could not account, and the knowledge of the practices of Sir Reginald, made me apprehend some murderous mischief; and the terror it must occasion you, my dearest Gertrude, determined me to put an end immediately to these impostures; and, by the assistance of Motley, I came, as you know, to the castle, in the character of an exorcist, or magician, qualified by my art to remove the disturbances raised by this ghost.

" Motley supplied me with a horse, which he took unperceived from the stable, and pursuing my way to ——, I purchased the habit necessary to my appearance

pearance in my new character of a magician. With this and my beard, with the addition of a conjur r's cap, which pretty well conceal d my face, my disguise wa so complete, that I could not even have known myself; I had therefore li'tle fear of being detected till my business was concluded.

"Thus, my dear Gertrude, have I given you a brief recital of all that passed both before and since my arrival on our Northern borders; what else remains to be known (continued the Baron) may be gained from Winifred, who, as well as Sir Reginald, is, at present, detained a close prisoner in the castle."

CHAP.

CHAP. VII.

True love's the gift which God has giv'n,
To man below, beneath the heav'n;
It is not fantasy's hot fire,
   Whose wishes soon as granted die;
It liveth not in fierce desire,
   With dead desire it doth not die.

SCOTT.

THE Baroness listened with surprise, and the most tender interest, to this affecting and extraordinary narration; and mingled tears of grateful joy in her pious ejaculations to Heaven, who had so wonderfully and unexpectedly reunited her to the object of her first and only love. The Baron,

Baron, while he folded her to his heart, seemed to enclose in his arms the treasure of a world. Often as he gazed on her did the tear steal into his eye, while with the enraptured glances of a lover, he viewed her perfect form, and beautiful face, to which a shade of sorrow had, without detracting from its loveliness, added a most affecting interest.

To feelings such as these, no language can do justice. Those only who have experienced them, can imagine the sensations thus mutually inspired: They were such as those feel who have been suddenly raised from the brink of misery, to the highest state of human happiness and enjoyment.

Lord Ormond, who had really felt a fraternal interest in every thing that could concern the Baroness, was not an unmoved

unmoved spectator of that felicity of which she so largely partook. With all the generous good-will of an honest soldier, he congratulated the Baron on his return. " My Lord," said he, " I sincerely wish you joy ; and that I think you must have it in the possession of such a woman as the Baroness your wife, is most evident, from the eagerness with which I myself sought her hand, while I thought it might be won with honour. Nor, my Lord, can your return be considered by me as the slightest reason for disappointment. I cannot for a moment regret that the Lady to whom I offered my suit, is the wife, and not the widow of Baron Fitzwalter. Before your arrival, my Lord, I was fully convinced she never would be mine. Her rejection of me, at a time when she was driven almost to frenzy, by

tho

the fears excited by this ghost, rendered
it impossible for me to doubt that her
attachment to you was not to be shaken
even by your death. For this I could
not but respect her, as even more than
woman; and though I checked my love,
it raised my admiration of her, and a wish
to do her service.

"Nothing, I thought, could answer
this my purpose more effectually, than an
investigation into the alarming affair of
the ghost; and suspecting some villany
was afloat, I hoped to discover whether or
no my suspicions were well grounded, by
spending a night, and meeting the apparition in the haunted chamber.

"With these opinions, my watch was
not a proof of extraordinary courage; but
when my sword broke, I confess I was
astonished; the effect seemed supernatural;

ral; and I followed the ghost with that persuasion; and in so doing, I confess I found I did it at the hazard of my life. It consoled me, however, in the midst of all the perplexities I experienced in the dark vaults, to reflect, that whatever I might suffer was owing to a good intention, however frustrated, and a disinterested wish to do good, which is indeed the soundest principle of human action, and must afford satisfaction, even in disappointment and defeat.

" And now, my Lord (continued the Earl), again let me express my satisfaction on the return of your happiness; and, after the honour of kissing the hand of your fair Lady, the late object of my suit, I ask permission, on the morn of to-morrow, to depart in friendship."

" My Lord," replied the Baron, " your
sentiments

sentiments and your conduct equally reflect upon you the highest honour, and
claim the best regards and gratitude of
myself and my wife. On a foundation
such as you have now laid, shall be built a
solid superstructure of inviolable friendship; and every possible connection shall
unite the families of Ormond and Fitzwalter. To-day shall be a day of festivity, and you shall share the entertainment of my table, and behold how my
friends and vassals shall revel on my
return. Various arrangements will for
some time occupy my attention, and
when they are over, let me hope to be
revisited by the noble Earl of Ormond."

"It shall be so," replied Ormond;
"let us taste to-day the delights of
friendship."

The day was so spent; nor were the
thoughts

thoughts of the Earl, when he laid him down to rest, less gratifying than the pleasures of the day. No envious jealous reflections of his having been rejected by the Baroness, dipped his thoughts in bitterness. His soul was the abode of that tranquil satisfaction, which results from virtuous integrity and honourable intention. The next morning, early, attended by his train, he left the castle.

The Baron, who knew not that the Earl had intended to depart so early, rose with a wish to shew him every courtesy and attention, suitable to his situation and rank, on his departure; and hearing that he had already left the castle, he expressed much concern. But now the seneschal delivered to him a letter left by the Earl, and which the Baron expected would explain the reasons of his early departure.

ture. The letter was couched in the following terms :——

———

" *TO GEOFFRY, BARON DE FITZWALTER.*

" An affair of importance claims my immediate attendance at court. With your good leave, if so be that I succeed in the business that takes me hence, I purpose speedily to be back again. Let not the Knight, Sir Reginald, escape his durance in your castle ; neither think the duty rests with you, of calling him to account for the villany he has practised towards you and me. I hereby claim the right of proving him a traitor, base and vile. Be not offended that I offer myself the avenger of wrong in this manner, to decide by lawful combat the justness of my cause, by the extent of his villany.

villany. May Heaven have you, and
your spouse, in it special keeping.

"Your's,

"ORMOND."

———

The Baron, almost immediately after the
receipt of the Earl s letter, repaired to the
apartment in which Sir Reginald Hare-
land was confined. Never were shame
and guilt more strikingly depicted, than
on the countenance of Sir Reginald. The
sight of the Baron overwhelmed him with
confusion and embarrassment. He could
scarcely speak. He arose as he approached;
but his limbs seemed palsied; he reeled,
then leaned panting against the chair
from which he had arisen, and covering
his face with his hands, remained silent
and motionless.

His

His feelings were apparently most painful. The Baron, notwithstanding his full sense and conviction of the dishonourable and guilty part he had acted, could not utterly withhold his pity from a man who seemed to be suffering under the keenest remorse, occasioned at least by shame, if not of repentance.

The dread of shame was, perhaps, the cause of his present distress; for it was not to be imagined that one who, driven by passion to acts of enormity, and the practice of the basest artifices, to the utter violation of all the rules of honour and common honesty, should all of a sudden change his nature, and abhor the course which he had so steadily pursued. But whatever might be the cause of his distress, the Baron was too humane to add unnecessarily to the uneasiness and mortification

fication of his unhappy kinsman. Indeed, he dreaded the effects a sense of his degradation might produce upon a mind like that of Sir Reginald, whose natural vehemence of temper, unaccustomed to controul or restriction, might, if much irritated, drive him to some act of desperation, and even urge him to lift his hand against his life.

He deemed it, therefore, prudent to endeavour to calm the passions that reigned in his breast, and soothe his griefs by an assurance of his entire forgiveness, and a promise of a speedy enlargement.

Sir Reginald, who could not but be highly sensible of the Baron's lenity, falteringly expressed his thanks, adding, " It is more, much more than I deserve. Oh that my future life could atone for the past! but it cannot: in death only

H   must

must I seek a refuge from my present misery, and the well deserved disgrace that I know awaits me."

"Rather live," cried the Baron, "that you may prove yourself yet capable of actions truly honourable. The connection which unites our families arrests the arm of one who ought otherwise to claim further answer. Accept, therefore, my pardon: prepare, however, to meet, in warlike guise, the noble Ormond, who, unrestrained by tie of blood, challenges you to combat."

"Where is he?" interrupted Sir Reginald, impetuously; "yet only in the field will I meet him."

"He has departed," said the Baron, "but ere long, for so a letter he has left informs me, purposes to return. Till then, Sir Knight, you remain no longer a captive,

tive, though an inhabitant of this castle, where you will be well served and attended."

" Oh, Fitzwalter!" cried Sir Reginald, with a look of deep contrition, " that with your forgiveness I could recover also your esteem. Oh, what a friend have I lost! by my own fault too, my own folly."

" Do not deem it impossible but you may some time recover it," said the Baron, " though you must first give me proof that you deserve to have it. I too, in you, have lost a friend, a friend on whom I once thought I could never have placed too high a value. I have been deceived —cruelly deceived! nevertheless, on your return to a just and honourable line of conduct, my heart is again ready to acknowledge you; and to renew, in some

degree,

degree, at least, the now broken bond of friendship

"By my own sad experience," cried Sir Reginald, " I have discovered, *and from my own example let it be told*, that there is no happiness to be found in any path but that of rectitude and honourable integrity. Had I not deviated from these, I might still have known comfort; that self-approbation, and virtuous satisfaction, which results from good intentions, and well directed efforts for the attainment of what is really excellent and praise-worthy, would, at least, have been mine; and these, I now feel, would be happiness placed on the best and surest basis."

" Encourage these sentiments," said the Baron, "a nd fear not; should Heaven preserve you, you may yet attain it, secured as it will then be upon the best

and

and indeed only principle that can render it durable."

' Had success attended my endeavours," said Sir Reginald, " I should still, I think, have been wretched. Led on, step by step, through the violence of my own passions, to actions which I grieve to reflect upon, and which must for ever entail upon me disgrace and infamy, it seemed utterly impossible to stop, or measure back the path in which I trod. I could not, or I would not halt in my miserable career of guilty deception, even though the pang of remorse invaded my repose, and threatened constantly to pursue and torment me. Wearied with my confinement in the range of apartments allotted me, where I was obliged occasionally to skulk behind the arras or wainscot; degraded too, in my own opi-

nion,

nion, by the mean arts I was obliged to use for the prosecution of my scheme, I was more than once inclined to abandon it, and leave the castle with the same secrecy, and in the same disguise in which I had entered it, after my seeming public departure, before the arrival of Earl Ormond. Would to Heaven I had obeyed the impulse of these feelings! for then, at least, I should have escaped a part of the disgrace I have incurred."

As he uttered these words, Sir Reginald sighed heavily; and leaning upon the arm of his chair, remained silent, but agitated: in reply to some enquiries made by the Baron, as soon as he was sufficiently composed to be able to answer them, chiefly in relation to Earl Ormond's adventure in the chamber, he received at different intervals the following account.

Sir

Sir Reginald, when informed by Winifred, who was the only person in his secret, and from whom he received constant encouragement, that the Earl had determined to keep watch in the chamber, doubted not but he could deceive him, as he had done the rest of the inhabitants, into a belief that the castle was haunted; and this without any other trouble than that of practising anew the same manœuvres he had so often repeated with success; for he had no intention of shewing himself, or of executing the rash and daring scheme he afterwards projected, on finding the Earl was not easily to be caught in his snares, and might, therefore, if not properly secured, till the business was completed, expose both him and his designs.

A powerful soporific, which the Earl

had

had been artfully induced to take on his third night's watch, soon threw him into a sleep, the soundness of which gave Sir Reginald ample opportunity to effectuate his project.

He entered the apartment with the caution requisite to his purpose. He took Lord Ormond's sword, and departing by the way he came, hacked it in several places. He then poured upon it one of those liquids, which have the property of dissolving steel and other metals; this was the cause of its shivering to pieces, at the moment when the Earl attempted to strike.

Sir Reginald having thus convinced him that the appearance before him was more than human, Ormond, as has been already mentioned, followed him from the chamber through the mysteriously-con-
                                        structed

structed pannel, and in obedience to his
signals, descended the steps leading into
the lower vault. When there enclosed,
Sir Reginald knew he must have expected
to perish, but he was not so barbarous as
to design his death. It was his intention,
had Ormond not escaped himself from the
vault, to have decoyed him through a
door, communicating with a flight of
steps leading up into the northern turret,
and to have placed him in safety; taking
care, indeed, that he should not have the
power of returning, at least for some time,
to the inhabited parts of the castle. In
the meantime, his accomplice, Winifred,
undertook to supply him with necessaries
during his confinement.

To convey food, without allowing him
to suppose that it was done by human

means,,

means, was difficult; nevertheless, it was not altogether impossible but that they might deceive him. But, at all events, as he was now, for a time, at least, in their power, they resolved to run any hazard, rather than endanger the life and health of their noble prisoner.

His early release, accomplished, as it was, by the courage and intrepidity of the youth Edgar, would, in all probability, have opened the eyes of the family to a conviction that the ghost was an impostor, even if the Baron, assisted by the clown, had not discovered the trick, and exposed him to the Baroness, in the manner before described. Such are the troubles and hazards of villany. Sir Reginald was in constant dread of them; but he had now gone too far to recede;

and

and could only hope for safety, or success, by a perseverance in his desperate enterprize.

To have stopped short in his career of vice and folly, required, as Sir Reginald had himself observed, a degree of virtuous energy far beyond what he possessed, though, like most wanderers in the path of error, he had found it so intricate and full of mazes, that he was heartily weary of it. Besides, he was continually receiving fresh supplies of hope from his indefatigable agent, Winifred, who constantly assured him, that the most favourable effects imaginable were daily taking place in the mind of the Baroness, in consequence of their practices.

She even assured the Knight, that the Baroness was herself persuaded that the noises and appearances, of which she had

heard

heard so much, and by which she had been herself so greatly terrified and alarmed, were caused by the anger of this ghost on Sir Reginald's dismission, and at her reception of Earl Ormond; and that this persuasion had been farther confirmed, by her having heard, as she believed, the voice of the apparition, the sound of which seemed to issue from without the wall of her apartment, at a time when she was in deep conference with her confessor.

To the wall of this chamber Sir Reginald had contrived to gain access, without passing through the corridor, by means of the secret door by which Edgar and the fool had entered, into what was now called the haunted apartment, on the night that Ethelind was confined in it by Winifred.

Often

Often passing in and out through the pannel, which led to an unoccupied suit of rooms, where he lived secure and unmolested, Sir Reginald had already once shewn himself to this girl—a circumstance which excited so much terror and distress, that he resolved not to repeat his visit to the chamber, on the night of her confinement in it; and, had not Edgar been her companion, would not have proceeded so far as he then did.

An extraordinary dream, in which Sir Reginald thought he saw and conversed with the Baron on the subject of his marriage with the Baroness, caused perhaps by his mind's being continually occupied and engaged by these and similar ruminations, first suggested to Winifred, to whom Sir Reginald had imparted it, the idea of his appearing as a ghost. By an an artful relation, which she had partly fabricated for her purpose, Winifred prepared her Lady to receive what Sir Reginald, at her instigation, afterwards took occasion to unfold. This, though it bore some resemblance to the images presented in the dream, had but little foundation in truth; and Sir Reginald, recoiling with a sensation of shame and self-reproach from the mean stratagems he was obliged to use, could with difficulty be persuaded to impose upon the Baroness with this artful relation; after Winifred, with a happy imagination, had modelled and fitted it for the purpose on which it was to be employed. Nor would he have yielded to such a persuasion, from any arguments less powerful than those used by Winifred, who confidently declared it was impossible for him to succeed in his endeavours.

to

to win the Baroness, unless he could first
convince her that the marriage was necessary to the repose of her late Lord, and
that he had in some way signified this his
wish and desire. This was the ground-
work of a plan rashly formed, and on the
success of which all Sir Reginald's hopes
of obtaining the object of his wild pursuit seemed finally to rest.

From its purport, not less than the
mysterious obscurity in which it was
partly veiled, it was every way calculated
to make a strong impression upon the
mind of the Baroness—a mind too innocent for suspicion, and incapable, from its
very nature, of suspecting fraud or artifice
in others.

The Baroness did not entirely escape
the toil; she was, however, so far disen-
gaged as to be able to extricate herself
from

from the meshes artfully woven to entrap
her, ere, urged by terror and despair, she
had consented to sacrifice that liberty she
so highly valued, and those sentiments of
affection for her Lord, which it had been
long her pride and glory to entertain.

CHAP,

CHAP. VIII.

Then I am paid;
And once again I do receive thee honest——
Who by repentance is not satisfied,
Is not of heav'n nor earth.

SHAKESPEARE.

AFTER the confession of Sir Reginald, another of the culprits remained to be examined, namely, Dame Winifred, who, if she was not culpable in the same degree as Sir Reginald, had, nevertheless, to the great displeasure of the Baroness, been guilty of so many arts and impostures, in the pursuit of her own interest, as must naturally

naturally have precluded every hope of
being suffered to retain her present station
and authority.

Fully sensible of her enormities, though,
probably, without any sensations of real
penitence or sorrow, except such as were
excited by disappointment and disgrace,
it was with difficulty she was led into the
presence of the Baron and Baroness.

Winifred, once most absolute and
tyrannical over all the persons belonging
to the establishment, was now, in the situation of a fallen favourite, surrounded by
enemies.   Every act of injustice and op-
pression, which had attended the exercise
of her authority, was conveyed to the ear
of the Baron, either in open charges, or
indirect hints, but particularly in respect
to her conduct toward the orphan Ethelind, who, since her cruel confinement by
Winifred,

Winifred, in the haunted chamber, had been pitied, and much noticed by the Baroness, and on that account, whatever related to her seemed to admit of communication, without hazard, and even, perhaps, with advantage.

To these various accusations, indeed, except in the case of Ethelind, the Baron did not much attend. He knew enough to condemn her. Winifred was now as humble and depressed, as she had formerly been lofty and overbearing. Like all favourites, who never endeavour to gain the love of those over whom they domineer, she fell at once, and fell, like Wolsey, to rise no more.

At all times, her sole dependance was upon the favour and partiality of the Baroness; and, while cunning could serve, she secured it. But when the reason for

that

that was past, and of the good opinion of her Lady she had ceased to have any hope, she was ready to make as many confessions and concessions as were required, nay, even more; and particularly to cast all possible blame and odium on Sir Reginald Harcland.

Her accounts of the transactions of the castle differed little from those given by her accomplice, and were probably true. Indeed, falsehood, in the present situation of affairs, she soon perceived could afford her no subterfuge; for truth only could obtain credit, and prevent her falling into a deeper abyss of disgrace, than that into which her own avarice and folly had already plunged her. When she had ended the medley of her declarations, the Baroness thus addressed her :—

"I find, with the greatest concern and selfreprehension, that in you, Winifred, I have placed a culpable and most undeserved confidence. It has, however, taught me a lesson, which I hope never to forget. It has convinced me that there is no situation of life, however elevated, that can really exempt us from the performance of our domestic duties, or any feelings that ought to be suffered to interfere with them. Immersed in selfish grief, and rendered almost incapable of mental exertion, by the mental languor it had caused, I suffered many disorders, which I ought to have noticed, to pass unhindered and uncensured; and must therefore consider myself as in great measure accessary to them. I would not know, for I enquired not into the station of my dependant people, and could not, therefore, prevent them. But while I thus

blame

blame myself, I must not acquit you, or treat you as guiltless: you must no longer remain one of my household. My Lord has prepared for you a place on his estates, where, as a vassal, you will not be tempted to practise any abuses of your authority. You may now retire."

By the firm and dignified tone of voice in which these words were pronounced, Winifred found she had nothing now to expect from the former partial fondness of the Baroness. The recollection of this seemed only to inspire in her feelings of dissatisfaction and regret. She wept— she wrung her hands—she pleaded earnestly for forgiveness. The Baroness was not unmoved by the distress of her former favourite; but she was not to be diverted from her very proper resolution, and she was ordered to retire.

The

The steward, who had connived at Winifred's entertainment of the ghost, in
return for her connivance at his drunken-
ness and waste, was also placed, like Winifred, in the condition of a vassal, in one
of the Baron's villages; who thus fulfilled
his own prediction, made in the character
of a magician, that he would not be suffered to retain his stewardship many days.

Edgar, who had shewn himself inflex-
ibly honest, courageous, and humane, and
had been actively serviceable in several of
the late transactions at the castle, was
appointed to succeed him; and accordingly the next day received the wand of
his new office, and the furred gown, worn
on solemn occasions by the stewards of
the Lords of Fitzwalter.

As soon as Edgar was invested with
these badges of his office, he was led by
his

his benefactor into the apartment of the
Baroness, where she was sitting, attended
only by Ethelind. " With your good
leave, my Lady," said the Baron, " I
present, for your approbation and favour,
this the new steward and comptroller of
my household, one who has deserved well
of us; and will, I know, deserve still
more by future services."

Edgar, whose robust figure assumed a
very dignified appearance in his new
dress, bowed most respectfully; and the
Baroness, pleased with the manly address,
and ingenuous countenance of the young
man, received him with great condescension. She mentioned with thanks the
service he had performed in liberating the
Earl; praised his courage, in daring to
meet that phantom, which all the rest of
the family heard with fear, and presented
him

him with a large purse of gold.   She even
held out her hand to him to kiss, an honour which the new steward received with
proud gratitude on his knees.

"You have done us some service,
young man," said the Baron, "and we
are desirous to reward you : can we confer upon you any further favour?"

"My Lord," cried Edgar, stealing a
timid glance at Ethelind, who was seated
by the side of the Baroness.   He bowed
with a blush of honest sensibility, far
more expressive than any studied answer.

"I see," resumed the Baron, with a
benevolent and indulgent tone, "you
have yet something to desire ; and indeed,
something yet remains to prove my thorough acquaintance with the *arts of magi-
cal divination, and knowledge of the occult
sciences.* Words spoke by me then, I now

J   regard

regard as a promise. Here, take this sweet—this lovely flower," added he, leading the blushing, trembling Ethelind to her adored, her adoring Edgar; " I have gathered it for thee, keep it, and cherish it in thy bosom."

Edgar took the hand of Ethelind, thus presented by the Baron; tears rushed into the eyes of both; they dropped on their knees before the Baron, in lively, grateful, silent joy. He then, taking the hand of the Baroness, added, " My excellent Lady, let this meritorious couple be the objects alike of thy favour as of mine; I cannot frame for them a kinder wish, than that they may be as happy as ourselves."

Edgar and Ethelind were deeply affected by this kindness. Their hearts were too full to speak. It was a moment of transport;

port; but the finest luxury of feeling was not all their own; the Baron and Baroness shared it with them; and their own happiness was enhanced by the power they possessed of communicating good to those whom they esteemed.

The act of conferring kindness is the surest means of producing in the heart good-will and attachment: so true is it, that all our good qualities are improved, and almost created by practice. This was particularly confirmed in the Baroness, who now experienced an attachment to the fair orphan, which was hourly encreasing, and was hourly improved by acts of kindness and affection. She appointed her to the situation of the first of her female attendants, in the stead of the unworthy Winifred; and made her rich in presents from her wardrobe. She even

designed

designed the dress to be worn by the fair bride on the occasion of her marriage. This was a robe, made in the Spanish costume, fitted to the waist, so as to shew to advantage the beauty of her shape and figure, made open at the bosom, and with short slash sleeves fastened to a boddice with silver clasps, and adorned in embroidery with the richest pattern of needlework. Her fine light hair was to be braided, without any ornament, and tied up behind with a knot of natural flowers.

The Baron fixed the next day for the nuptials, and assigned them private apartments in one of the towers, which commanded a fine view of the lake, and also of the principal approach to the castle; and the happy pair immediately began, with the assistance of several of the domestics,

mestics, to order and furnish the rooms of their new abode.

In the morning, Ethelind, adorned less, perhaps, by the presents from her Lady's wardrobe, than by that expression of innocence and modest grace, which was so peculiarly her own, waited, attended by the happy Edgar, in the hall, the coming of the Baron and Baroness, who had most graciously promised to attend the solemnities at the chapel. As soon as they appeared, the fair bride, her lovely face half concealed with a veil, modestly thrown over it, proceeded thither, attended by all the female domestics of the castle in their best attire, and a long troop of the vassalage, among which were most of Edgar's friends and relations; Edgar himself appearing in his new garb, as steward of the castle.

I 3 The

The marriage ceremony, at which Father Osborne officiated, being concluded in the chapel, the Baron gave prizes of strength and agility, to be contended for by the young men among his vassals and attendants; and the Baroness, with the bride at her right hand, and all the women, sat, and beheld this sort of rustic tournament, often conferring additional rewards on such of the agile youths as particularly distinguished themselves. She proposed also prizes to such of the maidens as chose to contend in the race, and display those bodily powers, which, though the refinement of later ages perhaps may scorn, the policy of these ages did not discourage.

In the meantime, refreshments of the best kinds were plentifully distributed among the crowd, and added to the festivity

vity of the sports; and, the prizes properly assigned, all persons who had any
claim upon the hospitality of the castle
were feasted in the hall. Plentiful
draughts of hippocras, or ale, dealt out,
according to the rank of the guests, were
drank to the bride and bridegroom, ere
they retired; and the posset offered, and
other humorous gambols practised, by
their more intimate friends and acquaintance.

No one could be more happy on this
joyful occasion than Motley, by whom
Edgar was highly beloved. He sung,
and jumped about incessantly He seemed
almost mad with delight. He could not
restrain his raptures, or the wild expression
of them; he was even riotous in his mirth
and joy.

While the revelling vassals were feasting

themselves

themselves long after the sun had sunk into the west, a squire and page appeared, with trumpets and bugle horns, sounding before the gates, and announced the approach of some illustrious guest; and in less than ten minutes, Earl Ormond, with his attendant train of hnights and their esquires, alighted at the steps of the great hall.

The Baron advanced in haste to meet and welcome the return of his noble friend, his own people, in the meantime, hastily arranging themselves in due order, formed a line on either side the entrance. The Baron having received and returned the Earl's salute, accompanied him into the hall, when a message was sent to the Baroness, to announce the arrival of the Earl.

These ceremonies over, the Baron courteously

teously expressed his pleasure on the honour of his renewed visit, as also the regret he had suffered on his having so suddenly quitted his castle. Then alluding to the subject of the Earl's letter, given to him on his departure, " he hoped," he said, " the business, whatever it was, that had abruptly called him thence, had terminated to his satisfaction?"

" It has ended," said the Earl, " if not above my agreeable expectations, to my most sanguine wishes, as this may advise you:" he then gave a writing into the Baron's hand, and bade him read it; adding, with a smile, " you see it was no trifling affair which caused my precipitate departure from your most hospitable roof. May you both," said he, bowing solemnly, " share the blessings of Heaven, and the

holy

holy saints! and may prosperity attend both you and yours!"

The instrument bore the Royal signature, and was sealed with the King's seal. It contained, beside a free pardon, and reversal of the attainder of the Baron, a full grant of all the lands of the domains of Fitzwalter, to be from thenceforth held free of suit and service, by him, and his heirs for ever.

"Best and most generous of men!" exclaimed the Baron, rushing into the arms of the Earl, which were opened to receive him, "it is to you—to you I owe this wonderful, this unexampled deed of clemency."

"Overwhelm me not thus with your gratitude, my noble Fitzwalter," cried the Earl; "if you knew what pleasure I have

felt

3

felt in this opportunity of serving you, you would know the obligation is all my own; but if you think aught is due to me, let me be repaid in that which I esteem of most value, the friendship of yourself and excellent Lady." He then, hastily turning the conversation, enquired concerning Sir Reginald.

"Sir Reginald," replied Fitzwalter, "is still at the castle, though not a prisoner within its walls." The Baron then gave a hasty recital of what had passed between Sir Reginald and himself since his departure.

"'Tis well," said the Earl, "that he repents. But yet, honour, and what is due to my own rank and character as a peer, and an English soldier, demand that I should defy him to a trial of arms. To-morrow must decide his fate and mine."

mine." He was proceeding, but seeing the Baroness approach, respectfully advanced to meet her.

The Baron, with all the eagerness of lively gratitude, informed her of the purport of the writing brought by the Earl " Behold," said he, " Gertrude, our friend, and our benefactor! Oh, join with me to bless, while life remains, yes, till we both have seen our latest hour, the noble, the generous Ormond!"

The Baroness read ; then threw herself at the feet of the Earl. Tears of gratitude and joy streamed fast down her cheeks. " Best—most honourable of men !" exclaimed she : she could add no more; but her beautiful eyes spoke a language far more eloquent than tongue could utter.

The Earl, with a look of the most respectful, though tender admiration, hastened

tened to raise her from her posture; and then led her to her seat. The Baron pressed the hand of the Earl in speechless transport.

While thus engaged, Father Osborne appeared, and requested permission to deliver a message from the unhappy, but penitent Sir Reginald Harcland. The Baron bade him speak, and the friar delivered himself thus:

" My noble Lords, and most excellent Lady, as it is the most important part of the office of a priest to reclaim the wandering from their errors, I ventured to visit Sir Reginald Harcland, on purpose to remind him of the violations of duty he had committed, in disturbing a peaceful family, for the sole purpose of gaining unjustifiably his desired purpose. I had scarce communicated to him the object of

my

my visit, when he prevented what I had
further to say, by expressions of sincere
contrition and sorrow for the follies into
which he had unadvisedly plunged.

'I have,' said the good Father,
'asked, and obtained the pardon of Baron Fitzwalter; he is, indeed, as generous
as he is good; nor will he triumph insult-
ingly over a convicted transgressor. But,'
says he, 'I wait to deprecate the wrath
of another noble personage, whom, in my
practices, I have grossly abused—the Earl
of Ormond. In decoying him by my
false arts into the lowermost vault, I have
subjected him to a dishonour, which, I
know, as a soldier, he must seek to resent
in arms. To lift my arm against the life
of one whom I have injured, though in
my own defence, may be consistent with
the laws of knighthood; but seems in
reality

reality to me an aggravation of my of-
fence; and a gross violation of all the
rules of reason, and all the laws of my
God. Let me then be spared this fresh
enormity; let not my conscience be farther wounded; and let the Earl be told
these my reasons. He and the noble Fitzwalter will know that I shrink not from
the trial of arms from coward fears. They
know that I have fought in the field of
battle undaunted; and at many a just has
my address been proved, in pointing the
spear against the most adroit and noble
knights my adversaries. They will know
this; and will acquit me of all charge
against the purity of my honour. But
yet the Earl must call me to the lists, unless I receive the protection of the church.
His honour cannot else be satisfied. In
me, good Father, behold a true penitent;

let

let me be shriven at thy holy knee, and let me, as a penance, proceed a pilgrim straight to Rome. My presence in England will not then dishonour Ormond, offend the Baron, or disgust his beloved Lady. Absolve me, and then receive my vow, which I here promise, in the sight of God, and all his holy saints and angels, faithfully to perform.'

"On this, my noble Lords, and worthy patroness, I did not hesitate to do my duty. With many a tear and prayer the Knight repented; was absolved by the authority of Holy Church; and is now in sanctuary at the altar of Durham, under the protection of religion; and, with all convenient speed, proceeds to Rome. Such is my message: may it meet your favour!"

"Why, this sounds nobly," cried the Baron. "The conduct of Sir Reginald in

this

this business proves him an honest man, whatever be his follies."

"My duties," cried the Earl, "are here arrested. I must bow to the power of the church; and when I behold the beautiful, the accomplished, the peerless Baroness of Fitzwalter, I can pardon the extravagances, nay, the injuries, of a man, who tried so many stratagems to win her; and with this reflection, I, from my heart, forgive my enemy his wrong."

"If this resolve of Sir Reginald Harcland," cried the Baroness, "prevents a trial of arms between himself and our noble friend the Earl of Ormond, I am indeed right glad of heart that he has thus determined and acted; and I cannot be sufficiently thankful to you, holy friar, for the part you have taken, and for the power of holy mother church, to prevent the

the mischief that might have ensued, from a suitor of one so unworthy as my-self. We have all reason then to be thankful; and all may learn from the events lately happening in Fitzwalter Castle, that integrity and virtue can alone afford happiness; and that dishonest cunning, though it may for a time disturb and dis-tress some few undeserving of suffering, yet it is always most afflictive to itself; and as it seldom can attain, so it never can enjoy the success it madly seeks."

" Your remark is indeed most just, my beloved Gertrude," said the Baron, "and well might it be, would men read such lessons as these, and gather the wisdom they are calculated to teach. But it is time our noble guest took some refresh-ment and repose; and when to-morrow comes, we will strive to do him honour, by entertaining

entertaining him in a manner suitable to his rank ; and in the midst of our revels, it will not fail to delight us much, to re-member the adventures of the minstrel, ghost, and *conjuror*."

Accordingly, on the following day, a splendid entertainment was given at the Castle of Fitzwalter, in honour of the Earl's arrival, which was graced with the presence of troops of knights and ladies, accompanied by all the vassalage of the domain of the barony. The guests dined in the hall, on tables covered with the most delicious viands; and drank the healths of the noble pair, from out goblets of massive gold.

While engaged in the festivities of this occasion, another guest was announced. It was Lord Broke, who yet knew not of the return of the Baron; for the Baroness,

by

by whom he had been for some time hourly expected, anticipating the joy of his surprise on seeing him, had forborne to inform him of this extraordinary event.

The delighted astonishment of the good old Lord may be easily imagined, on beholding the Baron, his beloved son-in-law, whom he had long mourned as dead; but when, in addition to this unlooked-for happiness, he learned that through the influence of the generous Earl he had obtained not only a pardon, but the free grant of the forfeited estates of the barony, he burst out into transports of joy and gratitude.

In the course of a few years after the occurrence of the events our history relates, the favourite wish of his heart, that of living to see a continuation of the line of honourable ancestry from which he sprang,

sprang, was fulfilled by the Baroness having two sons, the elder of which was to succeed to the estates of the house of Fitzwalter; the younger, in right of his mother, to those of the barony of Broke.

The birth of these sons, Geoffry and Richard, were succeeded in some years by that of a daughter, who inheriting, together with her beauty, the virtues and accomplishments of her mother, at nearly the same age at which she had been united to the Baron, formed an alliance with one of the noblest families in England.

* * * * * *

Edgar received a liberal reward from Earl Ormond, who honoured him with great attention, for the service he had performed for him, in releasing him from the gloomy cell into which he had been decoyed; nor was the young Sicilian, of whom

whom the Baron's relation gave some
account; forgotten in the general distri-
bution of rewards among those by whom
they were merited.   He was invited, received, and retained in the Castle of Fitzwalter; and was maintained and treated
in it as one of the most valuable of the
Baron's friends.   Earl Ormond resumed
his visits to the castle as frequently as his
duties as a soldier and a statesman would
permit; and the most entire friendship
and affection continued to subsist between
him and the Baron and Baroness.

In the course of a few years after the
occurrence of the events we have related,
he married a lady of birth and great
beauty, who, in disposition, and the virtues of the mind, bore a near resemblance
to the Baroness.   Beside an amiable and
lovely wife, he was blessed with two children,

dren, a son and a daughter, the latter of whom formed an alliance with Geoffry, the elder son and heir of the barony of Fitzwalter; thus completing the wish of the Baron, that every possible connection should unite the families of Ormond and Fitzwalter.

FINIS.

Lane, Darling, and Co. Leadenhall-Street.

GOTHIC NOVELS

ARNO PRESS

in cooperation with

McGRATH PUBLISHING COMPANY

Dacre, Charlotte ("Rosa Matilda"). **Confessions of the Nun of St. Omer,** A Tale. 2 vols. 1805. New Introduction by Devendra P. Varma.

Godwin, William. **St. Leon:** A Tale of the Sixteenth Century. 1831. New Foreword by Devendra P. Varma. New Introduction by Juliet Beckett.

Lee, Sophia. **The Recess:** Or, A Tale of Other Times. 3 vols. 1783. New Foreword by J. M. S. Tompkins. New Introduction by Devendra P. Varma.

Lewis, M[atthew] G[regory], trans. **The Bravo of Venice,** A Romance. 1805. New Introduction by Devendra P. Varma.

Prest, Thomas Preskett. **Varney the Vampire.** 3 vols. 1847. New Foreword by Robert Bloch. New Introduction by Devendra P. Varma.

Radcliffe, Ann. **The Castles of Athlin and Dunbayne:** A Highland Story. 1821. New Foreword by Frederick Shroyer.

Radcliffe, Ann. **Gaston De Blondeville.** 2 vols. 1826. New Introduction by Devendra P. Varma.

Radcliffe, Ann. **A Sicilian Romance.** 1821. New Foreword by Howard Mumford Jones. New Introduction by Devendra P. Varma.

Radcliffe, Mary-Anne. **Manfroné:** Or The One-Handed Monk. 2 vols. 1828. New Foreword by Devendra P. Varma. New Introduction by Coral Ann Howells.

Sleath, Eleanor. **The Nocturnal Minstrel.** 1810. New Introduction by Devendra P. Varma.